A Christmas Carol

Patrick Barlow

Inspired by
the Christmas story by
Charles Dickens

A SAMUEL FRENCH ACTING EDITION

SAMUEL
FRENCH
FOUNDED 1830

SAMUELFRENCH.COM
SAMUELFRENCH-LONDON.CO.UK

ISBN 978-0-573-70386-7

www.SamuelFrench.com
www.SamuelFrench-London.co.uk

FOR PRODUCTION ENQUIRIES

UNITED STATES AND CANADA
Info@SamuelFrench.com
1-866-598-8449

UNITED KINGDOM AND EUROPE
Plays@SamuelFrench-London.co.uk
020-7255-4302

Each title is subject to availability from Samuel French, depending upon country of performance. Please be aware that *A CHRISTMAS CAROL* may not be licensed by Samuel French in your territory. Professional and amateur producers should contact the nearest Samuel French office or licensing partner to verify availability.

MUSIC USE NOTE

IMPORTANT BILLING AND CREDIT REQUIREMENTS

PUBLISHER'S NOTE

A CHRISTMAS CAROL was first produced by the Delaware Theatre Company (Bud Martin, Executive Director) in Wilmington, Delaware on December 8, 2012. The production was directed by Joe Calarco, with sets by Brian Prather, costumes by Anne Kennedy, lighting by Chris Lee, sound by Victoria Delorio, puppet design by Thomas Getchell, and musical supervision by Mary-Mitchell Campbell. The Production Stage Manager was Brian V Klinger and the Assistant Stage Manager was Annie Halliday. The cast was as follows:

SCROOGE . . . . Andrew Long
ACTOR ONE . . . . Mark Light-Orr
ACTOR TWO . . . . Jessie Shelton
ACTOR THREE . . . . .Tina Stafford
ACTOR FOUR . . . . Steve Pacek

A CHRISTMAS CAROL was subsequently produced Off-Broadway at the Theatre at St. Clement's in New York City on November 25, 2013. The producers for the production were Terri and Timothy Childs and Rodger Hess. The production was directed by Joe Calarco, with sets by Brian Prather, costumes by Anne Kennedy, lighting by Chris Lee, sound by Victoria Delorio, puppet design by Thomas Getchell, and musical supervision by Mary-Mitchell Campbell. The Production Stage Manager was Michael Danek and the Assistant Stage Manager was Sara Sahin. The cast was as follows:

SCROOGE . . . . Peter Bradbury
ACTOR ONE . . . . Mark Light-Orr
ACTOR TWO . . . . Jessie Shelton
ACTOR THREE . . . . Franca Vercelloni
ACTOR FOUR . . . . .Mark Price

CHARACTERS

This play is written specifically for five actors. Three men and two women. One actor plays Scrooge throughout. Everybody else plays everybody else.

ACTOR ONE (M)

EBENEZER SCROOGE – Standard English – 50-60

ACTOR TWO (M)

BOB CRATCHIT – Cockney – 40
MARLEY – Standard English – 50-60
YOUNG SCROOGE – Standard – 16-19
LITTLE SCROOGE – Standard – 8
KATIE CRATCHIT – Cockney – 9
BOY IN STREET – Cockney – 12
FREDERICK'S CHILDREN – Standard – 3-12
VARIOUS NARRATORS, CAROL SINGERS, DEBTORS, SPIRITS, SKATERS, PIECES OF FURNITURE, GHOSTLY HELPERS, ETC.

ACTOR THREE (F)

MRS. LACK – Cockney – 40
LAVINIA BENTHAM – Standard – 35
MRS. GRIMES – Northern English – 60
FANNY – Standard – 18
ISABELLA – Sweet spoken Irish – 18-28
GHOST OF CHRISTMAS PRESENT – Cockney/Music Hall/ Various – 60
MARTHA CRATCHIT – Cockney – 16
FREDERICK'S HOUSEMAID – Cockney – 30
VARIOUS NARRATORS, CAROL SINGERS, DEBTORS, SPIRITS, SKATERS, PIECES OF FURNITURE, GHOSTLY HELPERS, ETC.

ACTOR FOUR (F)

HERMIONE BENTHAM – Standard – 35
GHOST OF CHRISTMAS PAST – Standard – 40
CONSTANCE – Standard – 30
MRS. CRATCHIT – Cockney – 40
SCROOGE'S MOTHER – Standard – 40
VARIOUS NARRATORS, CAROL SINGERS, DEBTORS, SPIRITS, SKATERS, PIECES OF FURNITURE, GHOSTLY HELPERS, ETC.

ACTOR FIVE (M)

FREDERICK – Standard – 35

MR. GRIMES – Northern English – 60

MR. FEZZIWIG – Irish – 50

GEORGE – Standard – 30

PETER CRATCHIT – Cockney – 14

ABIGAIL CRATCHIT – Cockney – 10

URSULA CRATCHIT – Cockney – 12

TINY TIM – Cockney – 8

GHOST OF CHRISTMAS YET TO COME – Standard – 50

PASSER-BY – Cockney – 20

VARIOUS NARRATORS, CAROL SINGERS, DEBTORS, SPIRITS, SKATERS, PIECES OF FURNITURE, GHOSTLY HELPERS, ETC.

SETTING

London

TIME

1842 and before and beyond

I have endeavoured in this Ghostly little piece to raise the Ghost of an Idea which shall not put my readers out of humour with themselves, with each other, with the season or with me. May it haunt their house pleasantly and no-one wish to lay it.

Their faithful Friend and Servant,

C.D.

December, 1843

INTRODUCTION TO THE SCRIPT

I hope the following thoughts may be of use to producers, directors, actors, designers and musical directors intending an involvement with this piece.

The play's most obvious immediate difference to most theatre versions of Dickens' *A Christmas Carol* is its minimal cast. Five actors play all twenty-five named characters, not including unnamed spirits, narrators, carol singers, ice skaters and, at various moments, Fezziwig's factory workers (about forty), the milling crowds of London Town (five hundred) not to mention the entire dispossessed of old England (several thousand).

While I'm thrilled if a smaller payroll helps you get the play on in these cash-strapped times, I would also suggest the very fact of having a minimal cast offers many exciting theatrical possibilities, not to say a chance to create real innovation and magic.

As a dramatist, I am most inspired and liberated by the great periods of simplicity in theatre: the Italian Commedia, the medieval Mystery Play, ancient Greek theatre, Shakespeare's Globe, where the story, the text, and the performer are central. This is why I like working with minimalist theatre – the theatre of bare necessities – and using the restraints it imposes. Putting the actor and the actor's skills – mime, mimicry, acrobatics, clowning, dramatic acting, dance, puppetry, mask work, music and singing – at the centre of the play in the service of the text and the telling of the story.

At the same time, just as the limitations of a small cast can work to your advantage, so too can the technical limitations of the space. Indeed it should be entirely possible to mount this play without any complicated technical equipment, with a minimum of props and costume, without wing space, fly tower, flying rigs (I will talk a little about flying later), even scenery. Not that these things are all bad. If you want them, use them. But the play shouldn't *depend* on them.

As I suggest in the bracketed stage directions on page 14 of the script, you could even try getting the actors to 'play' the set, using themselves as doors, door-bells, windows, beds, clocks, coat-hooks, etc. This is not essential but it would be interesting to experiment with this idea, and I have included some stage directions to reflect this. I particularly like the idea of the actors engaging with the set as a *reflection of Scrooge's story*, their involvement providing a kind of theatrical metaphor. They surround him, creating his physical world, but also reflect what's happening in his interior world too. At the start, as they dutifully build his Counting House around him, he is ruler of his kingdom, in control of his world. Not only people obey him, but the clock, the phonograph, the door-bell, the snow obey him. This is the world he has created, but the world, the dictatorship, of his mind too. His rule is all. Nothing threatens him. Everyone and everything in his thrall.

At the end, when we return with him to the same Counting House and he meets the Ghost of Christmas Yet To Come and his world spirals out of control, the actors are released from his regime. Their connection with him reversed and the tables turned. Now, despite his ranting and raving, they simply look on, offering no help, calmly and implacably allowing him to reap the rewards of his mis-spent, miserable and myopic life.

You will notice I have at certain points written quite detailed stage business, for example the 'human furniture' idea mentioned above. Needless to say I am not telling the director how to do her or his job. And there is no need to follow these exactly. I simply offer them as a hopefully helpful guide to what I was seeing as I wrote the play. The important thing is the story, the journey of Scrooge. From self-inflicted tyranny through the pain of revelation to ultimate liberation and true understanding.

However it is directed, I would certainly encourage the idea that all five actors are constantly employed throughout the show in telling the story. Even those not playing a character in a particular scene should be involved. Moving sets, holding windows, swinging doors, creating furniture, making sounds, playing violins, flying Scrooge, throwing snow, blowing trumpets, beating drums, whatever's to hand, whatever talents are available to weave the magic and keep the story galloping along. I would suggest an atmosphere of constant energy, inventiveness and presence should prevail.

Of course if your particular theatre has the wherewithal to create technical or visual magic, such as revolves or traps or flying rigs, then use them. Use whatever's available. In Joe Calarco's delightful, inventive and exhilarating production for the Delaware Theatre Company in 2012, and a year later at the

St Clement's Church off Broadway, his designer, Brian Prather, had the brilliant device of a central stage revolve with two spiral staircases on smaller revolves on top of the central revolve. This was a superb, indeed magical, way of getting Scrooge to fly and our producers Tim and Terri Childs made sure we had the budget to create it. It was a fabulous visual centre to the show and thrilling to watch nightly from my back seat in the auditorium. But the point is that nothing technical is *essential* to make the show work. And, however brilliant your design, don't let that take the pressure off your actors whose particular challenge is to appear – like magicians – to create a story out of nothing with nothing. 'Two trestles, two boards, and a little magic' as the old saying goes. Or something like that.

Talking of magic, in the early days of developing the script, our producers gave us the opportunity to investigate and workshop physical acting techniques with an initial team of actors under the thoughtful and inventive direction of Jeremy Dobrish and movement wizard Chris Bayes (who did the choreography on my *39 Steps* on and off Broadway). Over just a few days, we learnt with Chris magical ways of appearing, disappearing, making ghosts, creating snow and, most magical of all, how to fly, using just a chair, a sheet and a bucket. Magic is perfectly possible, and possibly preferable, using the simplest of means.

Finally a word about music. You will see from the ensuing script that I have specified particular Christmas songs and carols and English and Irish folk songs. I would say the carols and folk songs mentioned in the play are as essential to the piece as the text itself and I would put in a plea that they are used as suggested. As to the incidental music, I have written cues into the text for various classical pieces (e.g. "Lieutenant Kijé" by Prokoviev, Shostakovich "8th Symphony", Benjamin Britten "Fantasia", etc., even some modern movie soundtrack music (quite a bit from *Batman Begins!*). I know these will still be in copyright so almost certainly too costly to use so I offer them as a guide and reference only for specific cues and for the type or tone of music I had in mind as I was writing the play.

Besides *A Christmas Carol* and *The 39 Steps*, I am currently writing a four man *Ben-Hur* and have written and collaborated on a great number of minimalist shows for my company, The National Theatre of Brent, a two-man *The Charge of the Light Brigade*, a two-man *Zulu!*, a two-man *Life of the Bronte Sisters*, a two-man *French Revolution*, and a three-person Wagner's *Ring Cycle* to name but

ACT ONE

PROLOGUE

*(Four of our five **ACTORS** run on. They are dressed in Victorian hats, coats and mufflers. They look the very picture of Christmas card carollers. They launch happily into "DING DONG MERRILY ON HIGH". If they play musical instruments, all the better. They stop singing.)*

(Sound Effect: Distant tolling bell.)

ACTOR 2. Marley.

ACTOR 3. Jacob Marley.

ACTOR 4. Marley began it all.

ACTOR 5. By being dead.

ACTOR 2. Dead as a doornail.

ACTOR 3. And you can't get much deader than that.

ACTOR 4. Dead and buried in the graveyard he was.

ACTOR 5. The day before Christmas.

ACTOR 2. A year ago to the day.

ACTOR 3. The funeral witnessed by four attendants.

ACTOR 4. The clergyman.

ACTOR 5. The clerk.

ACTOR 2. The undertaker.

ACTOR 3. And the chief and sole mourner.

ACTOR 4. Ebenezer.

ACTOR 5. Obadiah.

ALL. Scrooge.

ACTOR 4. And that was the end of it.

ACTOR 5. Or was it?

SCROOGE'S VOICE. *(from the darkness)* Cratchit?

(The four **ACTORS** *freeze.* **ACTOR 2** *pulls on a threadbare muffler, becomes* **BOB CRATCHIT**.*)*

CRATCHIT. Yes sir Mr. Scrooge sir all ready sir!

Int. Scrooge's Counting House. Christmas Eve.
Dawn – Night.

(The ACTORS *jump to, rush offstage. Run back with Scrooge's Counting House which they create at breakneck speed. Doorway, shop-bell, Scrooge and Marley sign, coat hooks, clock, an ancient wind-up phonograph with a giant horn. The effect should be like a stage illusion, with the Counting House appearing as if from nowhere. [The* COMPANY *might consider using themselves, their bodies, as the set, adding to the sense that the actors themselves are somehow in* SCROOGE's *service (see Introduction).])*

(Lights change.)

*(*SCROOGE *appears. One minute he's not there, the next he is. Elegantly dressed in suit, cloak, bright waistcoat and top hat. Beaming brightly, he looks happily 'round his office.)*

SCROOGE. Everything tickety-boo Mr. Cratchit?

*(*CRATCHIT *takes* SCROOGE's *overcoat and and hangs them on hook [or* ACTOR*].)*

CRATCHIT. Everything tickety-boo sir yes thank you sir.

SCROOGE. Tickety-boo *for,* Mr. Cratchit?

CRATCHIT. Tickety-boo for er – *(thinks)* – the day sir?

SCROOGE. For the day indeed sir. Always for the day sir!

*(*SCROOGE *laughs.* CRATCHIT *laughs. The* ACTORS *laugh.)*

But for what else sir? What else *particularly* Mr. Cratchit are we tickety-boo for?

*(*SCROOGE *waits.* CRATCHIT *thinks. The* ACTORS *think.)*

CRATCHIT. Um –

SCROOGE. *(hums just audibly)* God rest you Merry Gentlemen –

CRATCHIT. *(small voice)* Christmas sir?

SCROOGE. What was that Cratchit? Didn't quite – catch it Cratchit!

(SCROOGE *laughs.* CRATCHIT *laughs. The* ACTORS *laugh.*)

CRATCHIT. Christmas sir!

SCROOGE. Christmas sir! Absolutely sir! Spot on Mr. Cratchit!

(SCROOGE *applauds. The* ACTORS *applaud.* CRATCHIT *bows.*)

CRATCHIT. Thank you thank you sir, thank you kindly sir!

SCROOGE. Now then! Eyes closed!

(CRATCHIT *and the* ACTORS *close their eyes.*)

SCROOGE. No peeking!

(SCROOGE *chuckles.* CRATCHIT *chuckles. The* ACTORS *chuckle.*)

(SCROOGE *pulls a cord. A garland drops down. It says* 'A PROSPEROUS CHRISTMAS TO OUR ESTEEMED CUSTOMERS'.)

SCROOGE. And open!

(CRATCHIT *and the* ACTORS *open their eyes. They see the garland [they've seen it before] and applaud wildly.*)

SCROOGE. Thank you, thank you, thank you. My mostest mostest favourite time of year. Is it not, Mr. Cratchit?

CRATCHIT. Indeed it is sir yes sir. Your mostest mostest, sir.

SCROOGE. Indeed indeed sir! Ha ha ha! Ho ho ho! So – let us begin on this happy happy Christmas Eve. Time please if you'd be so kind Mr. Cratchit?

(CRATCHIT *nods to the* ACTOR *playing the clock. The clock tings seven times.* SCROOGE, CRATCHIT *and the three* ACTORS *wait.*)

CRATCHIT. Seven o'clock sir.

SCROOGE. Seven o'clock. Precisely. And time for Mr. Cratchit?

MRS. LACK. Thank you sir. *(takes breath)* It's my husband sir you see sir. He's a good man sir, honest man sir. It's just – well there's no work sir and what with seven kiddies –

SCROOGE. Seven what – sorry?

MRS. LACK. Kiddies sir!

SCROOGE. Kiddies! *(chuckles knowingly)* Bit of a handful eh?

MRS. LACK. Oh yes sir. And what with it bein' Christmas –

SCROOGE. Did you say – Christmas?

MRS. LACK. Erm –

(He winks at **CRATCHIT,** *who winds and sets off the phonograph.)*

(Music [Phonograph]: "IT CAME UPON A MIDNIGHT CLEAR")

*(***MRS. LACK*** *looks enchanted.)*

SCROOGE. A blessed time indeed Mrs. Lack.

MRS. LACK. Oh yes indeed sir.

SCROOGE. Yet costly too methinks!

MRS. LACK. Oh yes sir, quite agree sir, yes indeed, indeed it is sir.

SCROOGE. Indeed indeedy Mrs. Lack.

(He laughs merrily. **MRS. LACK** *laughs,* **CRATCHIT** *and the* **ACTORS** *laugh.)*

So might I be correct in assuming a little advance might not go amiss?

MRS. LACK. *(not sure what he means)* Sorry – um – advance er –

SCROOGE. Lolly Mrs Lack!

MRS. LACK. Erm –

SCROOGE. Boodle! Spondulicks! Filthy lucre madam!

*(***MRS. LACK*** *still none the wiser.)*

SCROOGE. MONEY Mrs. Lack!?

(Music [Phonograph] Winds down)

MRS. LACK. Oh sir! *(stands and curtsies)* I wasn't wishin' to presume sir! But yes sir! Indeed sir! Thank you thank you kindly sir!

SCROOGE. Sit Mrs. Lack.

(She sits.)

'Tis nothing madam. 'Tis the duty of our trade after all. Us financiers. To help all those in need. That is what we are here for madam. 'Tis our sacred purpose. Is it not Mr. Cratchit?

CRATCHIT. Indeed it is sir.

MRS. LACK. *(shivering)* Thank you thank you sir!

SCROOGE. Cratchit!

CRATCHIT. Sir?

SCROOGE. Poor Mrs. Lack is shivering like a jelly in a hurricane! Light the jolly old fire, Mr. Cratchit!

*(**CRATCHIT** leaps off, returns with a roaring fire [or an **ACTOR** becomes the fire which **CRATCHIT** lights].)*

Nothing like a bit of jolly old warmth in the winter, eh Mrs. Lack?

MRS. LACK. *(rubbing her hands)* No indeed sir.

SCROOGE. So you see my dear lady you've come to the perfect person for your predicament. And with any luck Mrs. Lack you won't be Mrs. 'lack' any more! And all your little 'kiddies' will have full little tummies.

*(He laughs merrily. **MRS. LACK**, **CRATCHIT** and the **ACTORS** laugh merrily.)*

Mr. Cratchit if you please.

CRATCHIT. *(bows)* Very good sir.

*(**CRATCHIT** disappears off stage. He staggers back with an enormous box which he deposits heavily on the floor. **SCROOGE** takes a large jangling chain of keys from his waistcoat pocket. Finds the right key. Unlocks a padlock. Throws back the lid. A golden twinkling light shines out of the box.)*

(Music: "BARBASTELLA – 'BATMAN BEGINS'" soundtrack*)

(MRS. LACK, CRATCHIT and ACTORS creep forward and peer inside. MRS. LACK nearly faints at the sight.)

MRS. LACK. Oh my oh my sir!

SCROOGE. So what shall we say Mrs. Lack? A pound?

MRS. LACK. *(swooning with excitement) A pound!* A pound would be just – oh sir –

SCROOGE. Or how about – *(takes a handful of coins)* – five?

(He casually lets them drop back into the box.)

MRS. LACK. FIVE!!! *FIVE POUNDS SIR!!!* Oh my! Oh my! Thank you sir thank you!

(He picks out five coins. Proffers them to MRS. LACK who reaches eagerly for them. At the last moment, he clamps them in his fist.)

SCROOGE. At what shall we say? One hundred percent? How would that be?

MRS. LACK. *(not understanding)* One hun – um –

SCROOGE. Forgive me, I'm so sorry. Did I not explain? I am referring to the interest madam.

MRS. LACK. Erm – sorry –

SCROOGE. I can hardly lend you five pounds for nothing. Can I Mr. Cratchit? *Can I!?*

(He glares at CRATCHIT and the furniture.)

CRATCHIT & FURNITURE. No sir no sir!

SCROOGE. But – seeing as it's Christmas – how about – *(weighs it up)* – two? Hundred? Per cent?

MRS. LACK. *(utterly lost)* Two hun – per – oh! Thank you! No! What? Er –

(MRS. LACK stands. [The ACTOR/CHAIR stretches with relief.])

---

* Please see Music Use Note, p. 3

SCROOGE. *(pushes her down)* Sit Mrs. Lack!

> (MRS. LACK *sits hard on the* ACTOR/CHAIR. *[*ACTOR/
> CHAIR *gasps].)*

It's really very simple my dear sweet lady. Allow me to explain. I give you five shiny pounds from my big black box. You give me back – how much would Mrs. Lack give me back Cratchit? Cratchit!

CRATCHIT. *(sotto, hating this)* Ten pounds sir.

SCROOGE. Speak up Cratchit!?

CRATCHIT. Ten pounds sir.

SCROOGE. Ten pounds sir. Which on top of the five I loaned you comes to *(calculates)* fifteen pounds. In toto. Which you pay me – *(thinks about it)* – in a week. Okeydokey?

MRS. LACK. *Fifteen! In a wee – but HOW? – WHEN? How could I POSSIBLY –*

SCROOGE. *D'ye want the money or not!?*

> (MRS. LACK *looks racked.* CRATCHIT *keeps scribbling.)*

Oh well! If you absolutely insist!

(About to drop coins back in the box:)

MRS. LACK. No no no!!! Please sir please sir!

SCROOGE. Very wise decision if I may say so, Mrs. Lack! Now just a little tiny little signature if you'd be so kind. Thank you Mr. C?

> (CRATCHIT *brings paper and quill.)*

Just here please?

(She scribbles, CRATCHIT *reveals another paper.)*

And er – just here.

(scribbles, another)

And another little one.

(scribbles)

Thank you. And – er – here.

(scribbles)

And oh! One more just here.

(scribbles faster)

And – sorry! – another just here.

(even faster)

And one more.

(even faster)

And another.

(faster)

And the last one!

(faster)

And one more. *Quickly!*

(scribbles last signature)

And jolly good. Thank you, Cratchit.

(**CRATCHIT** *whisks away the papers and* **SCROOGE** *holds the coins up. He drops them one at a time into her palm.*)

SCROOGE. So Mrs. Lack! Five lovely jubbly poundies to you. Fifteen back to me. In – what was it? *(as if just remembering)* Ah yes! In a week.

MRS. LACK. *But sir! A week, sir! A week! Have a heart, sir!*

SCROOGE. Have a heart? *Have a heart!?* I've given you a whole week, madam! *(leans close and smiles)* Or I double it. Agreed? I said agreed!!??

MRS. LACK. Yes sir, yes sir yes sir.

SCROOGE. Splendid! There. That wasn't too painful, was it?

(**CRATCHIT** *winds the phonograph. Puts on a new cylinder.*)

(Music [Phonograph]: "JOY TO THE WORLD")

(**SCROOGE** *sings merrily along with the music.*)

SCROOGE. 'Joy to the world ba ba bum bum –' *(swings on* **MRS. LACK***)* Thank you, Mrs. Lack!

   (He slams down the lid of the chest.)

Good morning!

   *(***CRATCHIT** *opens the door.)*

   (Sound Effect: London street sounds.)

   *(***MRS. LACK** *throws snow over her head and exits.)*

   *(***CRATCHIT** *shuts door behind her. The bell [***ACTOR***] CLANGS.)*

   (Sound Effect: London street sounds. Cut.)

   *(***SCROOGE** *stops singing.)*

SCROOGE. Off Cratchit! Turn it OFF!!!

   *(***CRATCHIT** *turns off phonograph.)*

   (Music [Phonograph]: "JOY TO THE WORLD" cuts.)

SCROOGE. Splendid work Cratchit. *(claps his hands)* Fire out if you would please?

CRATCHIT. I thought a bit of jolly old winter warmth sir?

SCROOGE. Warmth makes one sluggish Cratchit. Can't have the staff sluggish can we Cratchit? Fire OUT Cratchit!

CRATCHIT. Very good, sir.

   *(***CRATCHIT** *puts out the fire. [Throws water over the* **ACTOR***?])*

   (Sound Effect: Steam sounds)

SCROOGE. Time Cratchit?

CRATCHIT. Twelve o'clock sir.

   (Nudges the **CLOCK.** *The* **CLOCK** *jumps to, starts to chime twelve.)*

CRATCHIT. *(brightens)* Lunchtime I believe sir.

SCROOGE. Lunch!

(**CRATCHIT** *pulls out a meagre lunch. The* **CLOCK** *and the* **ACTORS** *pull out meagre lunches.* **ALL** *start to eat.*)

SCROOGE. Faster!!

(*The* **CLOCK** *chimes and eats faster.* **CRATCHIT** *and the* **ACTORS** *eat faster.*)

SCROOGE. *FASTER!*

(**CRATCHIT**, **ACTORS** *and* **CLOCK** *even faster.*)

SCROOGE. Lunch over!

(**CLOCK** *does last chime.* **CRATCHIT** *and the* **ACTORS** *gobble down their lunches.*)

(*The shop door bell clangs.*)

(**SCROOGE** *and* **CRATCHIT** *freeze. Look at one another.*)

Another customer Cratchit! Ha ha!

CRATCHIT. *(riffles through appointment book)* Er –

SCROOGE. Splendid splendid! Chop chop Cratchit!

(**CRATCHIT** *runs for the door. Skids to a halt. Winds the phonograph. Juggles cylinders. Finds right one. Puts it on.*)

(*Music [Phonograph]: "WE WISH YOU A MERRY CHRISTMAS"*)

(*He opens the door.*)

(*Sound Effect: London street sounds.*)

(*Reveal* **FREDERICK**, *Scrooge's nephew.* **FREDERICK** *throws snow over himself.* **SCROOGE** *preens himself. Turns beaming.*)

Do come in why don't you? And to whom do I have the –

FREDERICK. My dear uncle Scrooge!

(*Marches in and slams the door. The bell [***ACTOR***] CLANGS.*)

(*Sound Effect: London street sounds cut*)

SCROOGE. *(face drops)* My dear nephew Frederick.

(SCROOGE turns off the phonograph.)

(Music [Phonograph]: "WE WISH YOU A MERRY CHRISTMAS" cuts)

And what can I do for you sir?

FREDERICK. You know full well sir what you can do for me sir!

(gives CRATCHIT his hat)

You can accept my invitation to Christmas dinner sir. Which I most earnestly proffer to you every year sir. To share Christmas Day with myself and my family sir.

SCROOGE. And the reply sir is the same as it is every year sir. No sir. Thank ye for the proffering sir and good day to thee sir.

(SCROOGE waits for him to leave. FREDERICK does not move.)

Have you not left sir?

FREDERICK. Why sir?

SCROOGE. Why what sir?

FREDERICK. Will you not come sir?

SCROOGE. Why will I not come sir? Because dear nephew – as I inform you every tedious year sir – I – veritably, utterly and indubitably HATE Christmas!!! And have no wish to share it with anyone! Least of all yourself or your – *wretched family sir!*

FREDERICK. So what is this uncle? *(He indicates the Christmas banner.)* And this sir?

(He winds up the phonograph.)

(Music [Phonograph]: "WE WISH YOU A MERRY CHRISTMAS")

A Christmas carol sir unless I am mistaken!

SCROOGE. This sir?

(SCROOGE snaps off the phonograph.)

(Music [Phonograph] cut)

SCROOGE. 'Tis the latest 'thing' in business sir if you wish to know sir. It is remarkably efficacious in separating credulous fools from their money and maximising profits. What do we call it Cratchit?

CRATCHIT. 'Marketing' sir.

SCROOGE. 'Marketing' sir. Not half clever eh? One day it will rule the world.

*(**SCROOGE** chuckles. **CRATCHIT** and the **ACTORS** chuckle uneasily.)*

But on no account allow its dreadful jollity to deceive you dear nephew. 'Tis all tinsel falsity, and means nothing sir. Like Christmas itself sir! Which you are welcome to! Good morrow sir and good riddance. Hat Cratchit! Door Cratchit!

*(**CRATCHIT** collects **FREDERICK**'s hat, runs to the door [**ACTOR**]. Opens it. The door-bell [**ACTOR**] clangs. **CRATCHIT** throws in a handful of snow.)*

(Sound Effect: London street sounds)

*(**CRATCHIT** waits, shivering by the door, holding out **FREDERICK**'s hat. **FREDERICK** marches to the door. Instead of leaving, he closes the door. The door-bell [**ACTOR**] clangs nervously.)*

(Sound Effect: London street sounds cut)

*(**SCROOGE** freezes.)*

SCROOGE. I said DOOR Cratchit!

*(**CRATCHIT** opens the door [**ACTOR**] again. Door-bell [**ACTOR**] clangs more nervously. **CRATCHIT** throws in more snow. Holds out **FREDERICK**'s hat.)*

(Sound Effect: London street sounds)

*(**FREDERICK** does not move. **CRATCHIT** shivers at the door. The door [**ACTOR**] shivers. The door-bell [**ACTOR**] shivers. **CRATCHIT** throws in another handful. **FREDERICK** takes the door knob.)*

FREDERICK. Sorry Mr. Cratchit.

(Shuts the door.)

(Sound Effect: London street sounds cut)

SCROOGE. *Did ye not hear me Cratchit!?*

*(***CRATCHIT*** reaches for the door-knob.)*

CRATCHIT. *(to* **FREDERICK***)* Sorry sir.

*(***FREDERICK*** takes the door-knob.)*

FREDERICK. *(to* **CRATCHIT***)* Sorry sir.

*(***FREDERICK*** holds the door [***ACTOR***] closed. **CRATCHIT**,
door and bell [***ACTORS***] FREEZE in terror. **FREDERICK**
turns on* **SCROOGE.***)*

FREDERICK. And will ye not hear *ME* sir! A Christmas feast
uncle! A roaring fire sir! A fine plump turkey sir!
Chestnut stuffing! Roast potatoes! Cranberry sauce,
brussel sprouts and gravy sir!

(He addresses this to **SCROOGE** *who stands grimacing,
but also to* **CRATCHIT***, the door [***ACTOR***] and the door-
bell [***ACTOR***] who listen yearningly.)*

CRATCHIT/DOOR/DOOR-BELL. Graaaaavy!!!

SCROOGE. *Gruel sir!!!!*

FREDERICK. No sir no! A true Christmas table uncle! All
alight with smiling faces! Joy on every countenance!
Music and dancing and –

SCROOGE. – and parlour games I should imagine sir!!!

FREDERICK. Yes uncle yes! All manner of games sir! O
uncle dearest uncle!!

(puts his arms round him)

SCROOGE. *(freezes)* Unhand sir me please sir!

(An awkward moment. **FREDERICK** *lets him go. Looks
at him.)*

FREDERICK. What *IS* it about Christmas uncle!? What is it
makes you so unhappy sir?

SCROOGE. *IT DOES NOT MAKE ME UNHAPPY SIR!* I am exceptionally happy with Christmas if you wish to know sir! It brings me joy sir! For the plump profits it heaps upon my table! For the merry way it stuffs my wallet sir! Christmas? I ADORE IT SIR!

FREDERICK. Profits uncle! Stuffed wallets sir! That is not the point of Christmas! Christmas is not that! It is a time of loving sir! Of giving and forgiving and –

SCROOGE. That is YOUR Christmas sir! Giving and forgiving and lovey dovey doving and *that* Christmas sir is a fraud! A sham! A fake sir! Just like this – paper *chain* sir! *(He rips down the banner.)* What is the excellently expressive and – if I may say so – hilarious word I use for 'Christmas' Cratchit? *CRATCHIT!!*

CRATCHIT. *(inaudible)* Humbug sir.

SCROOGE. Louder sir!

CRATCHIT. Humbug sir!

SCROOGE. Louder!

CRATCHIT. HUMBUG SIR!!!

SCROOGE. HUMBUG SIR!!!

FREDERICK. No sir! Not Humbug sir!! 'Tis the opposite sir! 'Tis an honest true good time sir! Meant for the honest *GOOD* of people. A merry time sir! Full of cheer! When all the world is glad sir!

SCROOGE. Cheer! Glad! Good!! Honest! Merry!!! Urgggggh! I tell thee if I could work my will nephew, every buffoon who goes about with 'Merry Christmas' on his lips and wastes his hours of righteous toil spreading Christmas cheer to all and sundry, making silly Christmas feasts and singing silly Christmas songs and playing *silly pathetic paltry parlour games,* would be boiled with his own Christmas pudding and buried in his grave with a stake of Christmas holly through his heart! Good day sir!

FREDERICK. I cannot believe uncle – that *somewhere* inside you, resides not a memory – a tiny spark of light glowing in your heart – when Christmas was a goodly time to you too sir! When you could say with an open heart, with all the world, God bless it! God bless it everyone!

CRATCHIT. *(applauds)* God bless it every one!

SCROOGE. *CRATCHIT! Get thee gone with thy blessings, sir!!!*

(**CRATCHIT** *freezes with fear.*)

One more sound from you sir and you'll keep your Christmas by losing your situation! I can snuff you out Cratchit. Like a candle Cratchit. Or a moth Cratchit. Just like – *(clicks fingers)* that Cratchit!

FREDERICK. I beg of thee sir –

SCROOGE. What!!!?

FREDERICK. Come for your sister then! For my dear mother's sake!

SCROOGE. *(turns on him)* Thy mother sir!? She is long gone sir! Did you not hear me nephew? I think thine ears are sealed sir!! *Nothing will induce me to come, sir! NOTHING!!!*

FREDERICK. But my wife sir! My darling Constance! My children sir! They long to meet you sir!

SCROOGE. *No-one longs to meet me sir! NOW BE GONE SIR!!!*

FREDERICK. This shell that entombs thee uncle! Like a dark cave sir! Why sir – why why –

SCROOGE. *WHY DID YOU GET MARRIED SIR?*

(*All freeze.* **CRATCHIT** *freezes. Even* **SCROOGE** *freezes.*)

FREDERICK. What?

SCROOGE. What?

FREDERICK. Why did I get –

SCROOGE. Nothing sir!

FREDERICK. Because I fell in love.

SCROOGE. *Love! Ha! LOVE!!??*

(*The shop door bell CLANGS.*)

(*All freeze.* **CRATCHIT** *riffles through his appointments book. Rushes to the window. Peers through it.*)

CRATCHIT. Two ladies sir!

SCROOGE. Ladies!!? *Ladies!!?* Quickly Cratchit quickly!

(**CRATCHIT** *winds the phonograph.* **SCROOGE** *plumps his tie, flounces his hair, smoothes his eyebrows.*)

(*Music [Phonograph]: "JOY TO THE WORLD"*)

(**FREDERICK** *stands there, as they run round him.* **CRATCHIT**, *still furiously hunting through his appointments book, rushes for the door [ACTOR]. Opens it.*)

(*Sound Effect: London street sounds*)

(*Reveal* **LAVINIA** *and* **HERMIONE BENTHAM**. *They throw snow over their heads.* **SCROOGE** *switches on his instant smile.*)

My dear ladies! Doooo come in if you would please!

(*The* **LADIES** *enter.* **CRATCHIT** *shuts the door [ACTOR].*)

(*Sound Effect: London street sounds cut*)

LAVINIA/HERMIONE. Thank you sir most kindly sir.

SCROOGE. Coats Cratchit!

(**CRATCHIT**, *still clutching his book, takes their coats, takes them to the coat hook [ACTOR]. [Realises the coat hook has now become* **LAVINIA**. *She won't hold her own coat so* **CRATCHIT** *now holds the coats himself.]*)

LAVINIA. And to whom do we have the honour? (*to* **FREDERICK**) Mr. Scrooge or Mr. Marley sir?

SCROOGE. (*steps in front of* **FREDERICK**, *bows*) Ebenezer Scrooge at your service ladies. Mr. Marley is...no longer – (*a stifled sob*)

(**CRATCHIT** *prepares the hanky.* **SCROOGE** *prepares to take it.*)

HERMIONE. My dear dear Mr. Scrooge sir!

(*She touches him tenderly.* **SCROOGE** *freezes. An awkward moment. She removes her hand.*)

(Music [Phonograph] winds down)

*(**SCROOGE** regains his composure.)*

SCROOGE. Charmed I'm sure ladies. Charmant as the French would say. Mesdames.

*(They all laugh politely. **CRATCHIT** puts away the hanky.)*

So anyway let us – er – *(He brightens.)* – cut to the chase shall we? A little Christmas loan perhaps? Mr. Cratchit?

*(**CRATCHIT** picks up loan papers and quill. Also juggles the appointments diary and the coats. Re-winds the phonograph.)*

HERMIONE. A loan?

SCROOGE. Or two possibly? Two little Christmas loans perhaps?

HERMIONE. No no sir. You mistake our purpose. We come for your charity sir.

*(**SCROOGE** stops beaming. **CRATCHIT** stops winding.)*

SCROOGE. My what?

LAVINIA. Charity sir? For the poor, the needy, the destitute, all who suffer at this Christmas tide.

(Sound Effect: Distant sounds of London Town)

SCROOGE. Are there no prisons?

HERMIONE. Prisons?

SCROOGE. Or workhouses? Are the Treadmill and the Poor Law not in full vigour?

HERMIONE. They are indeed sir. I wish I could say they were not.

LAVINIA. So – what may we put you down for?

SCROOGE. Down for?

FREDERICK. Down for uncle? *(takes out some coins)* Here madam. 'Tis not much. But it is something.

LAVINIA. Oh! Thank you sir, thank you kindly sir! Most generous sir!

(They all turn to **SCROOGE***.)*

HERMIONE. Sir?

*(***SCROOGE** *looks at them.)*

SCROOGE. Nothing.

HERMIONE. Ah! You wish to be anonymous.

SCROOGE. I wish to do my business madam. I help support the prisons and the workhouses if you care to know. And those who are 'poor and destitute' as you call them must simply go there and be quiet about it. And if they are too *WEAK* to go there madam, then they had better die without delay. And decrease the surplus population. Do us all a favour. Sorry ladies but this is the way the world is made and that is that. Boo hoo hoo but there we are. Good night ladies!

(The **BENTHAMS** *stand frozen.)*

I said GOOD NIGHT LADIES!

(He bows. The **BENTHAMS** *hastily grab their coats from* **CRATCHIT***. A jumble of coats as* **CRATCHIT** *opens the door for them.)*

(Sound Effect: London street sounds)

(The **BENTHAMS** *tumble out and exit.* **CRATCHIT** *runs after them, throws snow after them. Returns to the Counting House.* **ACTORS** *return as door and bell.* **CRATCHIT** *shuts the door [***ACTOR***].)*

(Sound Effect: London street sounds cut)

FREDERICK. I am sorry for thee uncle.

SCROOGE. Keep your sorrow for yourself sir.

FREDERICK. If you could listen to your own heart dear uncle –

SCROOGE. My heart sir? My heart ceased to beat many years ago sir. Cratchit!

*(***CRATCHIT** *opens the door [***ACTOR***]. Bell [***ACTOR***] CLANGS.)*

(Sound Effect: London street sounds)

(CRATCHIT gives FREDERICK his hat. FREDERICK exits. CRATCHIT waits. FREDERICK returns. CRATCHIT throws snow over him. FREDERICK exits. CRATCHIT shuts the door. Disappears into the shadows.)

(Sound Effect: London street sounds cut)

(Music: "SHOSTAKOVICH 8TH SYMPHONY – 4TH MOVEMENT" 0:0-0:14*)

(SCROOGE stands brooding in the gathering darkness.)

(Music: Builds)

(CRATCHIT creeps forward, cap and muffler in hand.)

(Music: Fades)

CRATCHIT. Sir? Excuse me sir?

SCROOGE. *WHAT!!?*

CRATCHIT. If it's – quite convenient sir –

SCROOGE. Convenient sir? For what sir!?

CRATCHIT. To bid you goodnight sir.

SCROOGE. Goodnight sir!? *GOODNIGHT SIR!!?* No it's not convenient sir. Not convenient one jot sir!

CRATCHIT. But sir it's – closing time sir.

CLOCK: *(forgotten his cue)* Sorry! *(dings eleven times)*

SCROOGE. Closing time! Closing time! It's always *closing time* isn't it! *(He looks at the clock dinging. Sighs.)* Get on with it!

CLOCK. *(Speeds up. Dings faster and faster.)* Sorry sorry! *(Loses count. Slows down. Goes faster. Gives up. Collapses exhausted.)*

SCROOGE. *(Turns to CRATCHIT.)* Go on then! Away with ye! Back first thing tomorrow!

CRATCHIT. *Tomorrow sir!?* But it's Christmas Day, sir!

SCROOGE. So what am I supposed to do Cratchit! While you're gallivanting with your brood. With all your loathsome little 'kiddies'! Gorging yourselves on some profligate Christmas bean-feast no doubt!

*See Music Use Note, p. 3

CRATCHIT. Yes sir. Sorry sir.

SCROOGE. Which I shall be paying for sir! Picking a man's pocket every twenty-fifth of December! It's not fair sir! But don't think about me, no no no, don't spare a thought for others will you! You wait sir! See how I work you next year sir! You'll *REPENT* sir then sir I can tell ye! Back on Boxing Day Cratchit! Before the first light cracks the sky! Or – it's the hatchet Cratchit!

CRATCHIT. Right sir.

(*Brings* SCROOGE*'s cloak, hat and stick. Puts cloak round him, over:*)

SCROOGE. So if you happened to have any little happy family jaunt jotted in your diary for that particular day Cratchit, then you'd better scratch it Cratchit! (*laughs loudly*) Ha ha ha ha ha!

CRATCHIT. (*laughs half-heartedly*) Very good sir. Yes sir. And a very happy –

SCROOGE. *EXIT CRATCHIT!*

(CRATCHIT *runs out. Remembers. Runs back. Throws snow over his own head. Runs out.*)

(*The other* ACTORS *disappear too.*)

(SCROOGE *stands all alone now. He peers through the window.*)

(*Sound Effect: Distant excited shrieks and cries of children*)

Look at 'em all! Little *kiddies!* Snowballing and tobogganing and – *skating!* How I hate *SKATING!*

(*shouts*) I hope the ice breaks! Hope it snaps and cracks beneath yer! Hope you *SKATE YOUR WAY TO HELL!*

(*Music: "SUICIDE GHOST – 'SIXTH SENSE'" soundtrack**)

(He turns, sees his chest of money, flings open the lid. The golden light shines up into his face. He thrusts his hands into the coins. They tumble through his fingers.)

(talks to the coins:) You won't run out on me will you? You won't desert me? We are safe together you and I. Are we not? We cannot be parted! Not ever!

(shouts up into the flies) And you! Ha ha!! Can't get your hands on it now can you, you old devil! 'Cos you're dead and buried Jacob Marley! Dead as a doornail! And you can't get much deader than that! Ha ha ha!

(Slams down the lid and locks the padlock tight with his jangling keys.)

(Music: Fades over)

*(**ACTORS** offstage sing: "THE COVENTRY CAROL". **SCROOGE** starts as he hears it. He creeps to the door and opens it. Reveals **CAROL SINGERS**.)*

CAROL SINGERS.
LULLY, LULLAY, THOU LITTLE TINY CHILD,
BY, BY, LULLY, LULLAY.
LULLAY, THOU LITTLE TINY CHILD.
BY, BY, LULLY, LULLAY.

*(They notice **SCROOGE**. They peter out nervously. **SCROOGE** approaches them. Appears to be taking out his wallet. Reveals a stick instead. He charges them, waving his stick and shouting.)*

SCROOGE. Gaaaah!!! Gaaaah!!!

*(The **CAROL SINGERS** scatter and disappear screaming.)*

Ext. London Streets. Christmas Eve. Night.

(Music: "PROKOVIEV – LIEUTENANT KIJÉ: TROIKA"*)

(Sound Effect: Loud London street sounds. Horses hooves, trundling coaches, barrel organ, people excited, selling wares.)

ACTOR 3. And so on that Christmas Eve, Ebenezer Scrooge locked his premises and wended his way home.

ACTOR 5. Past the bright lights of shops he went.

ACTOR 4. Full and glowing with sweetmeats and holly sprigs and bright red berries.

ACTOR 2. And mince pies and plum puddings, and boiling hot chestnuts –

ACTOR 5. And sausages and suckling pigs and the greatest white feathered turkey ever seen on any Christmas Eve in the great memory of Christmases!

ACTOR 3. But Scrooge – as he made his lonely way home –

(Sound Effect and Music stop.)

– saw none of it.

(Music: Intro and First verse: "CAROL – THIS IS THE TRUTH FROM ABOVE" [Vaughan Williams – "Fantasia on Christmas Carols"**] [This could also be sung by **COMPANY***.])*

(Slow fade to black.)

---

*Please see Music Use Note, p. 3
** Please see Music Use Note, p. 3

Scrooge's Bedroom. Christmas Eve. Night.

(Lights come up. **SCROOGE** *sitting alone in bed in nightshirt and nightcap, in one hand he holds a single candle illuminating his face and in the other a meagre soup bowl.* **SCROOGE** *hears the carol. He stands, marches to the window.)*

SCROOGE. *QUIETTTTT!!!!!! INFERNAL RACKET!*

(He slams the window.)

(Music cuts out.)

(Sits back in bed again. Slurps noisily from his soup bowl. The other **ACTORS** *are* **SPIRITS** *in the shadows or offstage.)*

(mimics **FREDERICK***)*

Oooh! Christmas uncle! Visit us for Christmas uncle Scrooge! Christmas Day with Constance! Darling Constance! Constance and the family! Constance and the family! Oooh!! Constance Constance Constance Constance!

(Slurps his soup. Mimics **HERMIONE.***)*

And ooooh Mr. Scrooge sir! Remember the poor and the destitute! All lonely at Christmas Time!

(Slurps his soup. Mimics **CRATCHIT.***)*

And oh Mr. Scrooge sir, if it's all the same with you sir? I have to go home to Mrs. Cratchit sir and all the little snatchit Cratchits sir, if you're sure sir, if it's quite conveeenient sir? Well it's not sir! Not conveeenient! Not conveeeenient at all sir!

(Sound Effect: Scraping chain sounds)

*(***SCROOGE** *looks up. Listens. Goes back to his soup. Another slurp. It tastes disgusting. He spits it back in the bowl.)*

Yuk!!! Plain wicked is what it is sir! D'ye hear me sir!!??

(Sound Effect: Chain sounds. Louder.)

(He looks up again. Looks behind him. Continues slurping.)

(Sound Effect: Chain sounds)

SPIRITS. *(offstage) (whisper whisper)* Scrooge... Scrooge... Scrooge...

(SCROOGE stops slurping, Calls into the darkness.)

SCROOGE. Hello? Who's that?

(He gets out of bed, crosses the stage. Holds out candle. Peers into the darkness.)

Who is it!!?

(Gives up. Turns to go back.)

Humbug!!

MARLEY VOICE. *(offstage)* Scrooge!

SPIRITS. *(offstage) (whisper whisper)* Scrooge... Scrooge... Scrooge...

(SCROOGE stops, spins round.)

MARLEY VOICE. *(offstage) Ebeneezer Scroooge!!!*

(Sound Effect: Chains)

SPIRITS. *(offstage) (whisper whisper)* Scrooge... Scrooge... Scrooge...

(SCROOGE freezes, wide-eyed.)

SCROOGE. Who's that!? I know that voice! Can't be! Hah! *(shouts into the shadows)* Who *IS* that!? *Who is it!!??* Come *OUT NOW!* Do you hear me!

MARLEY VOICE. *(offstage)* Ebenezer! Here Ebenezer!

(Sound Effect: Chains)

SPIRITS. *(offstage, whisper laughing)* Here Ebenezer! Ebeneeeezer heeeeeere! Heeeeeere Ebeneeeezer!!

(SCROOGE creeps towards the whispering and laughter, further and further into the shadows. He peers into the darkness.)

(Sound Effect: FLASH of thunder and lightning)

(A ghostly **FIGURE** *BURSTS out.)*

(Sound Effect: Shrieking banshees!!!)

*(***SCROOGE*** *shrieks. Rolls across the floor. Still clutching his candle.)*

Music: "SUICIDE GHOST" – 'SIXTH SENSE' soundtrack*]

SCROOGE. Get back sir! Get back I tell thee!! Who are you sir? Who are you? *Who are you sir!?*

(Sound Effect: FLASH of thunder and lightening)

(The **FIGURE** *transforms into* **MARLEY'S GHOST**.*)*

(Music: Continues over)

MARLEY. 'Tis I EBENEZER!!! Jacob Marley!! Returned from the grave sir!!!

SCROOGE. *(transfixed)* MARLEY!!?? Marley!!??? Returned from the – No no no sir! You are – ha ha ha! Not he sir! You are – as door as a deadnail. As dale as a door-ned. As ned as a nob-dod. I mean – you are – you are – *(steadying himself)* – an infection of the mind sir. Is what you are sir! Caused by a crumb of cheese, a fragment of underdone potato, an undigested piece of roast beef. Grave sir!? There is more of gravy than of grave about you sir! You are not he sir! *(He laughs loudly.)* Ha ha ha ha ha!!!

MARLEY. Then I shall prove it to thee that I am sir. Remember mine face sir? A face like ancient parchment it was said sir.

(The **GHOST** *reveals his face. He might undo the traditional* **MARLEY** *bandage. He might pull a mask off. Whatever he does, he shrieks into* **SCROOGE***'s face.)*

AGGGGGGHHHHHHHHHHHHHHH!

SCROOGE. *AGGGGGGHHHHHHHHHHHHHHH!*

---

*(**SCROOGE** ricochets across the stage. Staggers to his feet.)*

SCROOGE. No no no no sir!!! You will not frighten me sir with all your ghosty tricks sir! I am very sorry if thou art decomposing but it is hardly my problem. Put a brave face on it sir! *(He laughs.)* Don't go to pieces! *(laughs again)* Ha ha ha!

MARLEY. *(unmoved)* True. It is not your problem. Yet. But soon it will be. For you bear the same fetters as I.

SCROOGE. Fetters? What fetters?

MARLEY. These fetters.

*(**MARLEY** stumbles as if dragging a great weight.)*

(Sound Effect: Chains)

SPIRITS. *(wails and moans)*

SCROOGE. Lo! What is this thou wearest? A great – *(gasps)* CHAIN!!! Clasped about thy ghostly middle made of –

*(The **ACTORS** offstage make metal clanking noises and intone.)*

ACTORS. – cash boxes –

SCROOGE. – cash boxes!

ACTORS. – heavy keys –

SCROOGE. – heavy keys!

ACTORS. – padlocks and bolts –

SCROOGE. – padlocks and bolts!

ACTORS. – deed boxes wrought in heavy steel!

SCROOGE. – deed boxes wrought in heavy steel!

MARLEY. 'Tis the chain I forged in life Ebenezer. And attached to it, all the dreadful accoutrements of my trade! *OUR* trade Ebenezer! Of my own free will did I wear it. As do you sir.

SCROOGE. Me sir! I have no chain sir! Ha ha! *(A jaunty little twirl.)* I am chain-free sir!

MARLEY. Only at the end willst thou seest it.

SCROOGE. End? What end?

MARLEY. Thine end sir! Only then willst thou seest that which – I dost – *(confused)* – seest.

SCROOGE. And what ist thoust dost doest – *(confused too)* seest sir...precisely?

MARLEY. That thou art eternally and irrevocably trapped! As I am!

SCROOGE. Eternally trapped?

MARLEY. *(pedantically)* Eternally and *irrevocably* trapped! *(Comes close.* **SCROOGE** *flinches at the smell.)* Shall I tell thee why?

SCROOGE. I'd rather you didn't actually.

MARLEY. Because, dear Ebenezer, in the whole of our miserable lives, never once did we help a single solitary human soul without some profit attached to it!

SCROOGE. So?

MARLEY. SO? SO?!?? That is not why we are here sir! Upon the earth sir! That is not our sacred purpose sir! To gain. To profit. To make *MONEY* sir*!*

SCROOGE. *(laughs)* I believe it is sir.

MARLEY. *NO SIR! NO EBENEZER! To help others! That* is our purpose sir! That is our sacred duty sir! And now that I SEE that, I cannot fulfill it! I am powerless sir! I can help no one! *(sobs)* I cannot touch them! I cannot reach them! They cannot even *SEE* me! Old friend, I am come this night to save thee from the same fate.

*(***SCROOGE*** *listens for a moment, then laughs in his face.)*

SCROOGE. *Humbug sir!* My sacred duty is to myself sir! Help others!? *Ha!!!* Our only duty upon this earth is to survive Jacob. In whatever way we can. We have no other purpose sir!

MARLEY. *(sobbing) NOOOOOOOO!!!!!*

SCROOGE. Jacob! Pull yourself together man! *(laughs)* Sorry probably a little late for that now. Listen Marley! Your fate is your fate. And my fate is mine.

And I have nothing to be *SAVED* from thank you! So kindly leave me to the rest of my days. That I shall live out as I see fit. Thank you sir for your concern sir! –

(Runs to the window, flings it open. A wild wind blows in.)

(Sound Effect: Wind sounds)

SCROOGE. – but now OUT if you would please! *(tries to waft him out of the window)* Out sir out!! Whoosh! Whoosh! Away away sir!!

MARLEY. It is already decided sir.

SCROOGE. *(stops wafting)* What is?

MARLEY. Three ghosts will visit you. This very night.

SCROOGE. *Ghosts? WHAT GHOSTS!!?* From where sir?

MARLEY. From – from – *(not actually sure)* – where – ghosts come from. They have already taken flight sir.

SCROOGE. *Taken flight!!?* Send them back sir!

MARLEY. I cannot sir. The first cometh at the last stroke of twelve. The second, at the third stroke of three expect. And the third at the second cock crow that doth herald forth the dawn.

SCROOGE. What?

MARLEY. *(sighs)* The first cometh at the first – last stroke of twelve. The second on the last – first *(confused)* – third stroke of three expect. And the third – heard upon the second – um – cock-crow that doth herald forth – doth forth – *(totally lost)* – the first – fourth – second – fourth of dawn. Got that?

SCROOGE. *What!? NO!!!*

MARLEY. Now I must leave thee sir!

*(**MARLEY** wraps his head again, or puts his mask on.)*

SCROOGE. Wait! Wait Jacob!

MARLEY. Thimmm hmmm armmm hhmmm eeezzzmm!

SCROOGE. *WHAT!!?*

MARLEY. *(Sighs. Unties head, or takes mask off.)* This is your last hope and chance Ebenezer!

SCROOGE. Hope and chance to what?

MARLEY. Repent sir! Open your heart to humanity before it is too late!

SCROOGE. *REPENT!?* Open my heart to humanity!? I hate humanity!! So it's pointless them coming, these ghosts!!! Damn you Marley!!!

MARLEY. I am already damned sir. But you can be saved! Repent ye of thy life! Change thine ways! Beg forgiveness Ebenezer! Old friend! Before it is too late!

(The **SPIRITS** *make haunting sounds of grief and regret.)*

Lo! See them before you! All the lost and inconsolable souls! Lamenting and weeping in the eternal night!

(Music: "BATMAN BEGINS: VESPERTILIO"*)

(The **ACTORS**' *weeping becomes louder. They become the shapes of inconsolable spirits. They fly about the stage.)*

ACTOR 3. And at that very moment the black night filled with phantoms of all the lost souls, all who had lost their chance to help their fellows in life.

*(***SCROOGE** *gazes up as they fly past him.)*

ACTOR 5. And as Scrooge gazed upon all the lost souls, he recognised many from his own profession.

ACTOR 4. Bankers, brokers and surety men –

ACTOR 3. Loan men, bailiffs.

ACTOR 5. Factory owners too and politicians and leaders of men.

ACTOR 3. Indeed one whole government did he espy all enchain-ed together, calling out in eternal regret.

ACTOR 5. Forgive us!

ACTOR 4. Forgive us!

ACTOR 3. We only cared about ourselves!

---

*Please see Music Use Note, p. 3

ACTOR 5. All we thought of was – Number One!

ALL. Forgive us! Forgive us! Forgive us!

MARLEY. Don't become like them Scrooge! Change thine ways! Before it is too late! REPENT! REPENT!!!

(**SCROOGE** *gazes at the sight of the inconsolable spirits appalled but unyielding.*)

SCROOGE. *NEVER!!! I SHALL NEVER REPENT!! CHANGE!!???*

ACTORS/MARLEY. *Chaaaaange Scrooooooge! CHANGE!!! REPENT!!! REPENT!!! REPENNNT!!!*

SCROOGE. *HUMBUG HUMBUG HUMBUG!!!*

(*Music climaxes – cuts out*)

(*Blackout.*)

Int. Scrooge's Bedroom – Christmas Eve. Midnight.

(Lights fade up on **SCROOGE** *in bed. He is snoring. For a moment there is peace.)*

(Sound Effect: CHURCH CLOCK chimes twelve)

*(***SCROOGE*** *is shocked awake. He listens till it strikes twelve.)*

SCROOGE. What did he say? The first cometh at the last stroke of twelve? *(He looks around him. Listens. Calls out.)* Hello! Hellooo! Hah! Nothing! Twelve has struck and – nothing! It was all a dream! Three ghosts! Hah! There are no ghosts! Ha ha ha! *(calls again, bolder)* O ghost!? Ghost!? Nothing. Nothing at all! Ha hah! I said gho-ost! *(calls louder, does a little jig)* O ghosty ghosty ghosty!!!??? –

VOICE. Mr. Scrooge?

*(***SCROOGE*** *freezes. He scrabbles for his candle, fumbles to light it, holds it out, peers into the darkness. A face [***GHOST OF CHRISTMAS PAST***] appears behind him. Pale, immobile, unsmiling.* **SCROOGE** *turns. The face remains behind him. He turns back. The face is in front of him. The face is androgynous. Very quiet and still.* **SCROOGE** *shrieks.)*

SCROOGE. Who are you!!?

GHOST OF CHRISTMAS PAST. I am the Ghost of Christmas Past.

SCROOGE. Christmas what?

GHOST OF CHRISTMAS PAST. Past.

SCROOGE. Christmas past! What is that to me?

GHOST OF CHRISTMAS PAST. 'Tis the key to thee sir.

SCROOGE. I have all the keys I need thank you.

GHOST OF CHRISTMAS PAST. Not all sir. Come sir.

SCROOGE. Certainly not!

GHOST OF CHRISTMAS PAST. But you called me, sir!

SCROOGE. No I didn't!

GHOST OF CHRISTMAS PAST. *(mimics) O ghosty ghosty ghosty!!!???*

(The **GHOST** *SNAPS his hand on* **SCROOGE***'s wrist.* **SCROOGE** *screams.)*

SCROOGE. Ow! What are you doing!? Let go this moment!

GHOST OF CHRISTMAS PAST. 'Tis time sir.

SCROOGE. Time? Time to what?

GHOST OF CHRISTMAS PAST. To journey to thy past sir.

SCROOGE. Past!? There is nothing in my past! It's – it's past!

GHOST OF CHRISTMAS PAST. Then there's nothing to be afraid of is there sir?

(Music: "DARKSEEKER DOGS – I AM LEGEND"*)

SCROOGE. I am not afraid! Not a bit of it!

GHOST OF CHRISTMAS PAST. Then why art thou trembling sir?

SCROOGE. *(trembling)* I am not trembling. It is uncommonly cold suddenly as it happens and I am – I am – I am –

(The back wall of the set lights up. **SCROOGE** *gasps, shielding his eyes from the dazzling light.)*

Agggh! What is this – this LIGHT?

GHOST OF CHRISTMAS PAST. 'Tis thy light Mr. Scrooge.

SCROOGE. My light! I don't have a light!

GHOST OF CHRISTMAS PAST. Oh yes you do sir. It has been darkened long enough. And now must shine as it should.

SCROOGE. I have no wish to shine thank you!

GHOST OF CHRISTMAS PAST. Come along sir.

(The **GHOST** *pulls* **SCROOGE.** **SCROOGE** *shrieks.)*

SCROOGE. What are you doing! WAIT! I – I should warn you I am in my night attire and cap which

---

*Please see Music Use Note, p. 3

is hardly suited to exterior pedestrian purposes! Not to mention a slight head cold which I have in my – my head as it happens –

GHOST OF CHRISTMAS PAST. Come sir.

(She makes a mystic gesture. **SCROOGE** *leaves the ground.)*

SCROOGE. Aggghhh!!!! Wait! What are you –

GHOST OF CHRISTMAS PAST. There is much to be done sir.

*(***SCROOGE*** *starts to 'fly'. He shrieks again, eyes tight shut, as the* **ACTORS** *move the set.)*

SCROOGE. Heeeeelp!!!!!!

(Music builds.)

(Lights flash.)

Ext. Country Road – Christmas Eve.

(Sound Effect: Birds in hedgerows, far-off church bell)

(SCROOGE and the GHOST stand together. SCROOGE opens his eyes. Looks about him. Blinks. Gasps.)

SCROOGE. Where am I? Where is my house? My room? My bed? My bedposts? My bedsheets? What am I – *(gasps)* But wait! *(peers around him)* This place! I know it! It is –

GHOST OF CHRISTMAS PAST. Where we begin sir. On Christmas Eve.

(Sound Effect: Approaching carriage)

(The other ACTORS play BOYS on a horse-drawn carriage. They charge across the stage whooping and cheering.)

BOYS. Merry Christmas! Merry Christmas! Happy holiday! Happy holiday!

SCROOGE. I know these boys! *(calls to them)* Peter! Tom! Harry! Stop stop!

(They appear to pass through him. SCROOGE shrieks.)

They do not see me. Why did they not see me?

GHOST OF CHRISTMAS PAST. They have no consciousness of us sir. They are but the shadow of things that have been.

SCROOGE. I should have been on that carriage. It was going home for the holidays! Where was I?

GHOST OF CHRISTMAS PAST. Where were you Scrooge? Remember?

(Sound Effect: Single tolling school bell)

Int. Grimes Academy – Christmas Eve.

(**ACTOR 3** *pulls on [or becomes] a desk. She is also the voice of* **MRS. GRIMES**. **MR. GRIMES** *enters. Black frock coat with cane.*)

GRIMES. Scrooge?

SCROOGE. Mr. Grimes!

(*Enter* **ACTOR 2** *as* **LITTLE SCROOGE**, *aged eight. He is poring over an exercise book. [He could be a mask or puppet.]*)

GRIMES. I said Scrooge!

LITTLE SCROOGE. (*looks up, flinches*) Yes sir. Mr. Grimes sir.

GRIMES. I have heard from your father. He cannot take you home. So you must spend Christmas at the school.

LITTLE SCROOGE. Yes sir.

GRIMES. A burden and toil for me and Mrs. Grimes but there we are. Don't expect any Christmas jollities from us sir.

LITTLE SCROOGE. No sir.

GRIMES. No fine plump turkey sir! Chestnut stuffing, roast potatoes, brussel sprouts or gravy sir! Gruel will be thy fare sir.

LITTLE SCROOGE. Yes sir.

GRIMES. Ain't that right Mrs. Grimes?

MRS. GRIMES. (*offstage*) Gru-el! Quite right, Mr. Grimes!

MR. GRIMES. You have something to occupy you?

LITTLE SCROOGE. My mathematics sir.

GRIMES. Mathematics. Good.

(**GRIMES** *turns the pages with his cane. Whacks down with it.*)

Compound interest, boy! Compound! *Divide boy! Divide!*

LITTLE SCROOGE. Yes sir.

GRIMES. Stupid witless pointless child!

(He lashes the page as he shouts. **LITTLE SCROOGE** *flinches.* **SCROOGE** *flinches too. The* **GHOST** *quietly watches the scene, watches* **SCROOGE** *watching.* **GRIMES** *spots something else. Another book beneath the exercise book.)*

What's this?

LITTLE SCROOGE. *(tries to hide it)* Nothing sir.

*(***GRIMES** *nudges aside the maths book with his cane. He reveals hidden beneath it an old leather-bound volume. It is a story book. He turn the pages. Each one reveals a picture.)*

GRIMES. Robin Hood –

(turns page) Robinson Crusoe –

(turns page) Jack the Giant Killer!

(turns page) Ali Baba!! Open Sesame!??

(whacks the book) A STORY BOOK!!?

Paltry pointless *STORIES SIR!!?*

(whacks again) Where d'yer get this?

*(***LITTLE SCROOGE** *says nothing.)*

Speak up boy! Who gave it yer?

LITTLE SCROOGE. Don't remember sir.

GRIMES. Well we'll have a little look shall we?

(He grabs the book. Picks it up.)

LITTLE SCROOGE. No sir, please sir –

GRIMES. *QUIET!*

(turns first page) Ah yes. Here we are.

(reads) "This book is for you my sweet darling boy. A book of treasures for your life. And if I cannot –"

LITTLE SCROOGE. I beg sir, please sir!

*(***GRIMES** *leers into the* **BOY** *'s face.)*

GRIMES. O my sweeeet! My darling boy! My little treasure! Aaaaaaah! Little wussy pussy diddums! Who wrote this muck boy?

LITTLE SCROOGE. No-one sir.

GRIMES. Well they can't help you now can they boy? Wherever they are! Little pretty pictures! Little fairy stories! *(He whacks the desk.) FILTH!* Vile pointless *FILTH!!!* I'll give you "Open Sesame" boy.

(GRIMES holds the book up so LITTLE SCROOGE can see, then slowly and deliberately tears the book down the spine into two pieces. LITTLE SCROOGE and SCROOGE both flinch. GRIMES throws the pieces back on the desk.)

NOW GET RID OF IT!! Lock it away! Out of the light of day for ever!

LITTLE SCROOGE. Yes sir.

GRIMES. *(Whack!)* Again.

LITTLE SCROOGE. Yes sir!

GRIMES. *(Whack!)* Again.

LITTLE SCROOGE. Yes sir!

GRIMES. Good!

MRS. GRIMES. *(offstage) GRIMES!!!! Whatchoo doin' in there!?*

GRIMES. Coming my little petal. My little snowdrop. My little tiny little – *(chuckling fawningly)* – mousekin...

(To LITTLE SCROOGE) Gerron on wi' yer work, boy!

(GRIMES exits, chuckling and fawning.)

GHOST OF CHRISTMAS PAST. Do you recall this book Mr. Scrooge?

(SCROOGE says nothing.)

GHOST OF CHRISTMAS PAST. It looked beautiful.

SCROOGE. No memory of it.

GHOST OF CHRISTMAS PAST. Not the sweetest of men, Mr. Grimes.

SCROOGE. It's what I deserved. Made me the man I am sir.

GHOST OF CHRISTMAS PAST. Madam.

SCROOGE. Whatever you are.

(Music: ACTORS offstage sing "THE COVENTRY CAROL")

CAROL SINGERS.

> LULLY, LULLAY, THOU LITTLE TINY CHILD,
> BY, BY, LULLY, LULLAY.
> LULLAY, THOU LITTLE TINY CHILD.
> BY, BY, LULLY, LULLAY.

SCROOGE. *(starts)* What's that?

GHOST OF CHRISTMAS PAST. Just a Christmas carol sir.

SCROOGE. Yes I can hear that thank you! I'd like to go home now please.

GHOST OF CHRISTMAS PAST. We are sir.

SCROOGE. Good! About time!

GHOST OF CHRISTMAS PAST. To another home sir.

SCROOGE. Another home? What other home? I have no other –

GHOST OF CHRISTMAS PAST. Yes you do sir. Just eight years on sir.

SCROOGE. Eight years – ?

> *(***GHOST*** takes ***SCROOGE*** by the hand.)*

SCROOGE. Wait! No! I have no wish to – take me back to my – *(to ***CAROL SINGERS***) QUIET DAMN YOU!*

> *(***GHOST*** makes mystic gesture. Lifts him up.)*

SCROOGE. *Agggggghhhh!*

> *(***SCROOGE*** and the ***GHOST*** 'fly'.)*

SCROOGE. Wait! Not again! What are you

> *(***SCROOGE*** howls as they go higher and higher.)*

SCROOGE. *NO NO NO!!!*

> *(The ***COMPANY*** changes the set below.)*

> *(Music: "CORYNORHINUS" – 'BATMAN BEGINS"*)*

---

*Please see Music Use Note, p. 3

Int. Scrooge's Boyhood Home – Christmas Eve.

(**SCROOGE** *floats down and 'lands'. The* **GHOST** *beside him.* **SCROOGE** *panting with terror.*)

SCROOGE. That's the last time! The very last time you –

(**YOUNG SCROOGE**, *16, and* **FRAN**, *18, appear.* **SCROOGE** *freezes as he sees them. The* **GHOST** *watches him.* **FRAN** *whoops.*)

FRAN. Ebenezer! You're back!

(**FRAN** *runs and hugs* **YOUNG SCROOGE**. *She kisses him.*)

Oh I've missed you so!

GHOST OF CHRISTMAS PAST. Who is this? Scrooge?

SCROOGE. No idea. *(pulling away)* Need to go now.

GHOST OF CHRISTMAS PAST. *(pulling him back)* Your sister. Isn't it?

SCROOGE. Ow! What?

GHOST OF CHRISTMAS PAST. Your sister. Fran. Isn't it?

SCROOGE. Fran? Is it? No idea.

GHOST OF CHRISTMAS PAST. Next part of your story Scrooge.

FRAN. Oh Ebby Ebby! I'm so happy to see you!

GHOST OF CHRISTMAS PAST. How she loved you!

SCROOGE. Don't know what she's talking about! This is all pointless. Not my story! I hardly knew her.

YOUNG SCROOGE. How is father?

(**SCROOGE** *starts.* **GHOST** *watches him.*)

FRAN. He won't come down. I'm so sorry.

YOUNG SCROOGE. *(starts to go)* I'll leave then.

FRAN. *(chases him, holds him)* No no! Stay Ebby stay! Why does he do this? Why won't he see you?

YOUNG SCROOGE. Because I am no proper son that is why. Because I am indolent and should be seeking employment. I should be looking this very moment.

FRAN. It's Christmas Eve!

YOUNG SCROOGE. So?

FRAN. He will not blame you forever Ebby.

YOUNG SCROOGE. Well he should. It was my fault.

FRAN. It was not your fault! You were a baby!

YOUNG SCROOGE. It was my doing! It was the having of me!

(Pulls away. **FRAN** *clings to him.)*

FRAN. No no! Ebby Ebby!

YOUNG SCROOGE. I must go.

SCROOGE. We need to leave now please.

(The **GHOST** *grips his wrist tight.)*

Owww!

*(***FRAN** *holds* **YOUNG SCROOGE.***)*

YOUNG SCROOGE. Let me go!

SCROOGE. *(pulling at* **GHOST***'s wrist) Let me go!*

FRAN. *(suddenly)* Ebby! I could come with you! We could get away. Away from him.

(For a moment they brighten. Then sad again.)

How can I? He watches me like a hawk. I am not even allowed into the garden anymore. He lives in perpetual terror he will lose me too. That I shall die like she did. I know when he looks at me that's what he sees, that's what he fears. And I fear it too. If only I were stronger. I could come with you Ebby.

(She hugs him, holds him.)

I *could.* O Ebby! Dearest Ebby.

(They both know this is impossible. Her closeness becomes unbearable. He breaks away.)

YOUNG SCROOGE. This is pointless!

SCROOGE. Entirely pointless!

FANNY. I'm so sorry.

SCROOGE. This scene you've inflicted upon me!

FANNY. Don't hate me.

(**YOUNG SCROOGE** *looks at her, then turns and walks away. He disappears into the darkness.* **FRAN** *watches him go. She turns and disappears in the other direction.*)

SCROOGE. Pointless and irrelevant and entirely without purpose and we need to *LEAVE NOW PLEASE GHOST!*

GHOST OF CHRISTMAS PAST. What happened to her?

SCROOGE. It was all a long time ago. I really don't –

GHOST OF CHRISTMAS PAST. What happened Scrooge?

SCROOGE. She married, had a son. Then she died. That's all I recall.

GHOST OF CHRISTMAS PAST. Frederick.

SCROOGE. Frederick yes.

GHOST OF CHRISTMAS PAST. Your nephew Frederick.

SCROOGE. Yes. My nephew Frederick! What about him?

GHOST OF CHRISTMAS PAST. She died so young.

SCROOGE. These things happen.

GHOST OF CHRISTMAS PAST. You must miss her.

(*Sound Effect: Church clock starts to chime*)

Both of you.

SCROOGE. *Time!? Time!!? What's the time!!!?*

(*Sound Effect: Clock reaches six*)

SCROOGE. *Six!! Six o'clock! SIX O'CLOCK!!?? Cratchit!!? It's time, Cratchit! Time to count the money! Cratchit!*

(**SCROOGE** *runs round the stage.*)

Cratchit!!!

(**SCROOGE** *bumps into* **ACTOR 2** (**CRATCHIT** *and* **YOUNG SCROOGE**) *waiting for the next scene. Shouts into his face.*)

SCROOGE. *Cratchit! The money Cratchit!! The box Cratchit! Unlock the box Cratchit! CRATCHIIIIIT!*

(**ACTOR 2** *does not reply.*)

GHOST OF CHRISTMAS PAST. He cannot hear thee sir. He is beyond this realm sir.

(The **GHOST** *guides* **SCROOGE** *away.)*

We need to journey a while longer sir, before we can unlock the box sir.

SCROOGE. What!!? What journey? Journey where sir?

GHOST OF CHRISTMAS PAST. Madam.

SCROOGE. Madam!!

GHOST OF CHRISTMAS PAST. To another Christmas Mr. Scrooge. A merry Christmas sir.

SCROOGE. Merry Christmas!! Merry! Spirit!! Do You know nothing about me!!?

GHOST OF CHRISTMAS PAST. I'm learning, sir.

SCROOGE. Christmas is not merry! It can never be merry! It is *anathema* to me spirit! I loathe, hate and detest Christmas!

GHOST OF CHRISTMAS PAST. So we understand, sir.

SCROOGE. Good!!

GHOST OF CHRISTMAS PAST. Still it must be undergone. If we are to find the grail sir.

SCROOGE. The what?

GHOST OF CHRISTMAS PAST. Grail sir. Holy Grail.

SCROOGE. Holy –

*(***GHOST** *waves her hands.)*

(Music: Irish jig)

(The set dissolves and transforms into:)

Int. Fezziwigs Emporium – Christmas Eve.

(A large sign appears: 'FEZZIWIG'S ABUNDANT EMPORIUM – FOR ALL YOUR FAMILY PROVISIONS'.)

*(**MR. FEZZIWIG** appears. Rotund, jolly and Irish.)*

(Music: Builds)

FEZZIWIG. *Wey-hey!* Time for the Fezziwig Christmas party!

SCROOGE. *Fezziwig? Fezziwig!?* *(gasps)* I was apprenticed here! Old Fezziwig!

FEZZIWIG. Time for dancing and feasting and games and dancing and more dancing! And more dancing still! Come my little Fezziwiggers!

FEZZIWIG/3 ACTORS. Never was there such a feast as the Fezziwig Christmas Eve! Wey-hey!!!

*(**FEZZIWIG** and the two other **ACTORS** leap into the scene. They whoop, clap hands and change partners. The **GHOST** grabs **SCROOGE** and pulls him into the dance. **SCROOGE** resists but the **GHOST** is too strong.)*

SCROOGE. No! No! Stop it please! Stop it!

*(**SCROOGE** spins round with the **DANCERS**. They twirl excitedly round him. He sees them but they cannot see him.)*

(Music stops.)

*(The **ACTORS** skid to a stop. **SCROOGE** staggers dizzy and out of breath. He looks up and gasps. There in front of him is a girl. She is **ISABELLA**, 17. Radiantly beautiful.)*

Isabella!

FEZZIWIG. Change your partners please!

*(Immediately the **GHOST** bounces **SCROOGE** out of the way, while **FEZZIWIG** grabs **YOUNG SCROOGE** and puts him in **SCROOGE**'s place. **YOUNG SCROOGE** sees **ISABELLA**. He freezes with panic. Tries to escape.)*

YOUNG SCROOGE. I'm so sorry – I really have to – I'm sorry – I – I – really must –

(ISABELLA holds out her hand. Laughing. Irish accent.)

ISABELLA. Ebenezer!

YOUNG SCROOGE. – complete my – ledger – I'm sure someone else will be happy to – to –

FEZZIWIG. Ebenezer Scrooge!!

SCROOGE. Yes Mr. Fezziwig?

YOUNG SCROOGE. Yes Mr. Fezziwig?

FEZZIWIG. It's Christmas Eve my lad! Don't box yourself in boy! Don't be like young Marley who stays behind with his face of old parchment and his boxes and books and ledgers! There's a world out there don't you know! Stop all yer blessed counting boy!

YOUNG SCROOGE. Yes Mr. Fezziwig.

(ISABELLA waiting, smiling.)

FEZZIWIG. Besides that's my own blessed treasure stood before you Ebenezer! And she don't look at just anyone you know! Why, the angels fall from heaven just for a peek at her so they do! You goin' to dance with her or not boy?

YOUNG SCROOGE. *(to ISABELLA)* Would you – like to?

ISABELLA. It would make me happy sir.

(ISABELLA stretches her hand. YOUNG SCROOGE tentatively takes it. She shows him how to hold her. He finds this very difficult. FEZZIWIG beats time. SCROOGE and ISABELLA slowly start to dance, as FEZZIWIG sings:)

(Music: "RED IS THE ROSE (TRAD)")

FEZZIWIG. *(sings)*
COME OVER THE HILLS,
MY BONNIE IRISH LASS
COME OVER THE HILLS TO YOUR DARLING
YOU CHOOSE THE ROSE LOVE,
AND I'LL MAKE THE VOW,
AND I'LL BE YOUR TRUE LOVE FOREVER.

(Music: Continues INSTRUMENTAL)

(Round and round go **YOUNG SCROOGE** *and* **ISABELLA**. **SCROOGE** *watches them entranced. The* **GHOST** *watches* **SCROOGE**. *She whispers to him as they pass.)*

GHOST OF CHRISTMAS PAST. Do I see your foot tapping, sir?

SCROOGE. By no means!

GHOST OF CHRISTMAS PAST. My mistake. Sorry.

FEZZIWIG. *(sings)*
RED IS THE ROSE THAT IN YON GARDEN GROWS
FAIR IS THE LILY OF THE VALLEY
CLEAR IS THE WATER THAT FLOWS FROM THE SEA,
BUT MY LOVE IS FAIRER THAN ANY.

*(***YOUNG SCROOGE** *and* **ISABELLA** *spin round and round, increasingly enchanted with each other.* **ISABELLA** *tentatively kisses him.* **YOUNG SCROOGE** *very tentatively kisses her back. They kiss some more. They turn again. He takes a ring from his pocket. Nervously puts it on her finger. She smiles up at him. They kiss again.* **SCROOGE** *watches transfixed.* **FEZZIWIG** *comes to the end of the song. He fades into the shadows.)*

*(***YOUNG SCROOGE** *and* **ISABELLA** *gaze into each other's eyes. They stand frozen.)*

SCROOGE. A touching scene I'm sure spirit. But it served no purpose showing it to me. *(He claps his hands.)* Thank you! Thank you! That's enough thank you!

(They don't move.)

Why won't they move? Why won't they listen to me!?

GHOST OF CHRISTMAS PAST. They are in the past sir. And the past is immoveable.

SCROOGE. Well it's a relief it's over frankly.

GHOST OF CHRISTMAS PAST. 'Tis not over sir. Two years on if you would sir.

SCROOGE. Two years!?

GHOST OF CHRISTMAS PAST. To another scene. Another Christmas Eve sir.

SCROOGE. Another Christ – Spirit! Did I not just say –

(The **GHOST** *waves her hands. A mystic gesture.)*

(Sound Effect: Crack of lightning and thunder)

*(***YOUNG SCROOGE** *has vanished.* **ISABELLA** *standing on her own.* **SCROOGE** *watches.)*

Int. Scrooge & Isabella's Home. Christmas Eve.

(YOUNG SCROOGE marches on. He has grown grander. More stooped.)

YOUNG SCROOGE. Isabella? What is it?

ISABELLA. Ebenezer?

YOUNG SCROOGE. What?

ISABELLA. I have something for thee sir.

YOUNG SCROOGE. What?

(She holds out her hand. A flash of diamond.)

SCROOGE. Not this scene spirit. Not this Christmas!

GHOST OF CHRISTMAS PAST. I am afraid it must be borne sir.

YOUNG SCROOGE. Your ring.

*(She drops it in his hand. **SCROOGE** watches, frozen.)*

ISABELLA. It was my blessing, sir. But now I return it. *(closes his hand over the ring)* I fear you have another 'engagement' sir. That consumes your heart. Another passion sir.

YOUNG SCROOGE. Passion? What passion?

ISABELLA. All your gain sir! Your profits! Locking them up in your box every night of your life! That is your passion! Not *me* Ebenezer! I am not your passion! I am not your love! Where were you tonight?

YOUNG SCROOGE. Working!

ISABELLA. It is Christmas Eve!

YOUNG SCROOGE/OLD SCROOGE. *So!!??*

GHOST OF CHRISTMAS PAST. She cannot hear thee sir.

ISABELLA. 'Tis the day we met! The day you proposed!

*(Music: **CAROL SINGERS** in distance: "GOD REST YOU MERRY GENTLEMEN")*

YOUNG SCROOGE. What time have I for Christmas! I have to work! I have my customers to see to! My books to be balanced! I do it for us Belle!

ISABELLA. We were one beating heart Ebenezer. One. And full of joy. But now we are two and full of misery. How often and how keenly I have thought of this through the lonely hours of night I will not say to you. It is enough that I *have* thought of it and do think of it, and now – release you.

YOUNG SCROOGE. Release me!? You cannot release me!

ISABELLA. So leave your counting and your ledgers and your figures and your books and your *MONEY!* And come with me. For ever. With nothing! Just us!

(*YOUNG SCROOGE stares at her. An agony of indecision.*)

You cannot, can you?

(*Still* YOUNG SCROOGE *says nothing.* SCROOGE *watches spellbound.*)

Ebenezer?

(*still nothing.*)

It is said if a man follows not the true calling of his soul, his soul will turn black and bad. It will wither and die. I hope you are following your soul's true calling Ebenezer. And that your soul doth thrive. May you be happy in the life you choose sir.

(*ISABELLA turns and leaves. Both* SCROOGES *watch her go.*)

GHOST OF CHRISTMAS PAST. You did not stop her sir.

SCROOGE. For what purpose?

GHOST OF CHRISTMAS PAST. You had her heart sir!

SCROOGE. A distraction merely. A moment's weakness! A man must make his own way. He cannot afford such aberrations! She was a narrow escape if you want to know! That's all she was! (*He laughs.*) These – 'visions' do not touch me spirit!

GHOST OF CHRISTMAS PAST. Just one more if you would sir. Then I am done sir.

SCROOGE. *I am done with thee spirit!*

GHOST OF CHRISTMAS PAST. Not quite sir. Ten years forward sir.

SCROOGE. *Ten – !!! NO!!!*

(**GHOST** *waves her hands. Another mystic gesture.* **YOUNG SCROOGE** *walks into a pool of light, older, more stooped, more like* **SCROOGE,** *head buried in a ledger.* **SCROOGE** *stares at* **YOUNG SCROOGE**. *Their stance identical.*)

(*Music: Children singing "AWAY IN A MANGER"*)

If you would sir. *SIR!*

(*The* **GHOST** *pulls* **SCROOGE** *into the next scene.*)

SCROOGE. Ow!!

Int. Isabella's Home – Christmas Eve.

(Lights up on tableau. We see a **WOMAN** *sitting by a fire.)*

(Music: Singing continues)

SCROOGE. Now where?

(The **WOMAN** *stands suddenly. It is* **ISABELLA.** *Ten years older. She looks straight at* **SCROOGE** *and throws out her arms.)*

ISABELLA. Beloved!

*(***SCROOGE** *gasps.* **GEORGE** *appears behind him. Laden with presents.)*

GEORGE. My darling!

*(***SCROOGE** *spins round.* **GEORGE** *runs to* **ISABELLA.** *He appears to run straight through* **SCROOGE.** *He runs into* **ISABELLA***'s arms.)*

ISABELLA. Georgy! My darling darling!

(They laugh. They hug. They kiss. The presents fall around them.)

GEORGE. Where are the children?

ISABELLA. Listen.

(Singing: Builds)

GEORGE. Happy Christmas Eve my darling.

(He kisses her.)

ISABELLA. The day you proposed.

GEORGE. You remember?

ISABELLA. Every day I remember.

GEORGE. I was so nervous. I thought your heart might be elsewhere.

ISABELLA. Never sir.

(She kisses him.)

Never.

(**SCROOGE** *gazes at the scene. The* **GHOST** *watches him.*)

GEORGE. Belle.

ISABELLA. Yes?

GEORGE. I saw an old friend of yours tonight.

ISABELLA. Old friend?

GEORGE. I passed his office in the city. In Fetter Lane. Quite by chance. His partner Mr. Marley and he were counting their money. Heads bowed. Never once speaking. All the joys of Christmas Eve ringing in the streets around them. And they were sitting there. Oblivious. Like ghosts.

ISABELLA. He would have killed me George. Sure as light is light and snow is snow. If I had given him my heart. He surely would.

(*They take each others' hands. They kiss.*)

A narrow escape sir.

SCROOGE. Cratchit!!! The box Cratchit!!! Cratchit!!!

(*He runs into the wings, runs back. Bumps into* **ISABELLA** *and* **GEORGE.** *Sees they are still kissing. Shouts at them.*)

Cratchit! I need – Cratchit!!! *WHERE IS CRATCHIT!!*

(**ISABELLA** *and* **GEORGE** *are oblivious.*)

GHOST OF CHRISTMAS PAST. I have told thee sir. He is not here sir.

SCROOGE. Yes! I know that! *Alright! Thank you!!* I was just – just – *(gazing at them)* That's all she wanted! My heart! That's what she kept saying! *(mimicking, dances around them)* Your heart your heart! I hold you in my heart! Your heart is my blessing, Ebenezer! Oooh yes it is, Ebenezer! Your sweet tender heart, Ebenezer!

(**ISABELLA** *and* **GEORGE** *run out past* **SCROOGE.** *He shouts after them.*)

SCROOGE. *BLESSING!!?? BLESSING!!??* A heart is not a blessing! A heart is – but a – beating muscle! A beating ugly muscle that keeps us going! 'Til we drop. That is all it is and nothing more and that's an end to it! *(laughs uproariously)* Did you see *HIM! Ha!!!* Laden with gifts and Christmas humbug nonsense! Well he's welcome to her! They're welcome to each other! And to think I might have married her! Hah! HAH!! Good riddance spirit! I thought you were going to show me some important scenes! From my past! That – that one could – well – learn from and – and – could educate one – and – profit from and – and – but frankly – frankly they were – well frankly – *(He laughs.)* – a waste of time sir! A waste of precious time sir! Madam!!!!

GHOST OF CHRISTMAS PAST. Precious time indeed sir.

*(The **GHOST** vanishes. **SCROOGE** spins round.)*

SCROOGE. Spirit! Spirit!??

*(Looks for the **GHOST**. Runs round stage, runs off.)*

(offstage) SPIRIT!

(Runs back. Shouts up to the flies.)

You see! It hasn't worked has it!? I've defeated thee spirit! You've given up haven't you!? As I indicated to Mr. Marley at his attempted 'haunting', thy journey has been wasted! Repent me of my life!? Is that what you'd have me do? Well my life is mine own thank you! And I will do what I do with it and I will do it as I do it and THAT'S WHAT I'LL DO SPIRIT! So all your paltry pointless 'visions' are as dross! As chaff! As – as – bilge! I am unmoved! Undefeated! Unrepentant! Unchanged! Un – un – everything! *Ha ha ha ha!*

(He sings mockingly.)

God Rest You Merry Gentlemen, let nothing you dismay, da da da da da da da da da da da da! O Tidings of Comfort and Joy, Comfort and Joy, O tidings of comfort and blah blah blah blah blah!!!

(The **ACTORS** *appear behind him singing, playing instruments, beating percussion. They get louder and louder, more and more raucous.)*

(Music grows over this: "EVIL COMETH"*)

*(***SCROOGE** *holds his ears trying to drown out the sound.)*

(All music and sound cuts out.)

(Blackout.)

End Of Act One

---

* Please see Music Use Note, p. 3

ACT TWO

Int. Scrooge's Bedroom – Christmas Morning.

(Lights fade up on **SCROOGE** *in bed. He is snoring. The candle flickering beside him.)*

(Sound Effect: The church clock chimes.)

*(***SCROOGE*** *wakes with a start. The clock reaches the third chime. He listens.)*

SCROOGE. Third chime! Third chime? What did he say? *(remembering)* The second spirit on the third stroke of three expect!

(He looks around him. Lifts his candle. Peers round the room.)

Hah! There you see. Three strokes and nothing. Not a second spirit in sight! All a nonsense! Hah!

(calls out) Ghost of Christmas Past!? Helloooo! Very frightening! Oooooo! Told the other spirits not to bother I wouldn't wonder! Quick you ghosts! Back home to ghostyland! Let's find some other dupe to haunt! Ha ha ha! Beat you second spirit! Before you even got here!

(He disappears under the covers. We hear him chortling.)

Back to ghostyland! Ha ha ha ha! Ho ho ho ho! Ha ha –

(Stops chortling. Slowly turns over. Feels gingerly down the bed. Freezes. Peeks an eye out of the covers. Looks down. There is a huge shape in the bed. He shrieks.)

Agggghhhh!

69

*(The blanket flies off. A large jolly **LADY** bursts out: the **GHOST OF CHRISTMAS PRESENT**. Covered in tinsel, baubles, and bells.)*

GHOST OF CHRISTMAS PRESENT. (*Broad Cockney*) Hello darlin'!

SCROOGE. Aaaagggh!

GHOST OF CHRISTMAS PRESENT. (*counts time*) One two, one two three four!

*(The other **ACTORS** burst on to stage. They are her **SCRATCH BAND** with tambourine, tin cans, anything they can lay their hands on. They sing and play:)*

(Music: "JOY TO THE WORLD". Very jolly and fast, first verse)

*(**SCROOGE** shrieks, leaps out of bed, runs round the room. Tries to escape. Tries the window, tries the door. Crawls under the bed. **GHOST** and **BAND** chase him. They catch him. Pull him up. Dust him down.)*

GHOST OF CHRISTMAS PRESENT. Now where was we darlin'? Ah yes! Sorry I'm late dear. Still better late than never that's what I say! Gor blimey! You look a bit peaky! Got out of bed the wrong side darlin'?

SCROOGE. I haven't been to bed.

GHOST OF CHRISTMAS PRESENT. Oh no! That's right. So you ain't darlin'! You must be *EX-HAUSTED!* Betcha feel like a lovely long sleep!

SCROOGE. Well actually I –

*(The **SCRATCH BAND** burst into:)*

(Music: "JOY TO THE WORLD". Even jollier, faster, and louder)

SCROOGE. *AGGGGHHHHH!*

*(The **SCRATCH BAND** cuts.)*

GHOST OF CHRISTMAS PRESENT. Anyway – *(Mrs. Doubtfire Scottish)* – what about all that then? Oooo Mr. Scrooooge!! All them 'Christmases Past' darlin'? Spooky I'd say!

(The **BAND** *makes spooky sounds.)*

(Cockney again) Still all long gone and forgotten now thank goodness.

(Wicked Witch of the West. Peers at him.) Or are they?

(witchy cackle) Anyway –

(Cockney) – my turn now. Guess who I am darlin'?

SCROOGE. I've absolutely no –

GHOST OF CHRISTMAS PRESENT. The Spirit of Christmas Present dear! Of course!

(The **BAND** *strike up again. He runs again. They give chase again. Catch him. Push him on the floor. She takes a pose like a hunter.)*

Ta-da! Now then what happens is this see.

(Pulls him to his feet.)

Ready darlin'?

SCROOGE. No I am not! In fact I should like to make it quite clear –

GHOST OF CHRISTMAS PRESENT. *(Bronx accent)* Cut the gab, nightcap man, or you'll be swimmin' wid da fishies!

SCROOGE. What!!?

GHOST OF CHRISTMAS PRESENT. *(Cockney)* You do what I say now, darlin'!

SCROOGE. Absolutely not! I most –

GHOST OF CHRISTMAS PRESENT. *(mimicking earlier* SCROOGE*)* Did you not hear me sir? I think thine ears are sealed, sir!

(She boxes his ears.)

SCROOGE. Ow!!!

(She takes his hand. Becomes a Russian fortune-teller.)

GHOST OF CHRISTMAS PRESENT. O Scrooge, Scrooge, come with meee on a dark and dangerous journey to thine present Scrooge, so we can see how all them things thou didst in 'the then' has led to all them things thou doest in 'the now'. Or 'the present'. So to speak. Geddit?

SCROOGE. *(mystified)* What?

GHOST OF CHRISTMAS PRESENT. *(Cockney)* Course you do darlin'. Simple when you fink about it.

SCROOGE. What –

GHOST OF CHRISTMAS PRESENT. *(Italian maestro) SILENZIO!!*

(Whacks him round the head. Tweaks his nose.)

SCROOGE. Ow!!!

GHOST OF CHRISTMAS PRESENT. *(Cockney)* Whilst all the while accompanyin' me upon the blessed task for which I was born for darlin'! Just one day in the whole year dear. I only live this one special day then I am – guess what I am?

SCROOGE. *(blank)*

GHOST OF CHRISTMAS PRESENT. *(ghosty voice) – no moooore! (laughs)* But while I'm 'ere dear I'm 'ale and 'earty dear! Visitin' the world! And spreadin' – spreadin'? Yes dear!? Come on! *Come on!!!*

SCROOGE. What!?

GHOST OF CHRISTMAS PRESENT. Spreadin' Christmas cheer dear. *(tosses glitter over him)*

SCROOGE. *(splutters)* What is *THAT!?*

GHOST OF CHRISTMAS PRESENT. Christmas cheer dear. Get with the programme, darlin'!

*(The **BAND** strikes up with "Joy to the World". They chase him round the stage. **SCROOGE** hollers.)*

SCROOGE. *WILL YOU STOP YOUR UNGODLY RACKET!!!*

GHOST OF CHRISTMAS PRESENT. But it's Christmas, dear!!!

SCROOGE. *Madam!* – *(sotto)* You are a madam?

GHOST OF CHRISTMAS PRESENT. I should 'ope so darlin'! *(slaps him)* Cheeky!

SCROOGE. Ow!!! Perhaps – madam – I did not make myself crystal clear to your departed colleague – who I sent *packing* by the way! –

GHOST OF CHRISTMAS PRESENT. What dear?

SCROOGE. – that I – Ebenezer Scrooge – *HATE CHRISTMAS!* And anyone who –

GHOST OF CHRISTMAS PRESENT. *(very fast)* – wastes his hours of righteous toil spreading Christmas cheer to all and sundry should be boiled with his own Christmas pudding and buried in his grave with a stake of Christmas holly through his heart! Ain't that how it goeth sir?

SCROOGE. *(disconcerted)* Yes it is how it...goeth if you wish to – knoweth...and I am of that opinion still madam thank you! I do not see Christmas, I do not hear Christmas, I do not smell Christmas, I am oblivious to all Christmas!

GHOST OF CHRISTMAS PRESENT. Where d'yer live then, in a cave?

SCROOGE. Yes if you will, I do. I live in a cave of my own design and I'm very happy in it thank you. I know what you would have me spirit. You would have me *CHANGED!* But you will fail madam! I assure you of that! For I am –

GHOST OF CHRISTMAS PRESENT. Gawd you're a talker!

(grips **SCROOGE***'s wrist)*

SCROOGE. *Owww!!!*

GHOST OF CHRISTMAS PRESENT. *(recites, doggerel style)*

Come fly with me upon this day,

But a little time to pass dear.

Come let me lead thee by the hand,

Or by thy bony arse dear!

(She kicks his butt.)

SCROOGE. Owww!

(She tosses another handful of glitter at him. He coughs and splutters.)

'Cos what day is it today darlin'?

SCROOGE. *I have absolutely –*

GHOST OF CHRISTMAS PRESENT. CHRISTMAS DAY WHAT ELSE DARLIN'!

*(Big fanfare from the **BAND**. They all throw glitter over **SCROOGE**. **SCROOGE** splutters. The **GHOST** spins him round.)*

Come along dear! Wheeeee!

(She pulls him sharply. They take off.)

SCROOGE. *(shrieks)* Agggghhh!

(Music: "LIEUTENANT KIJÉ: TROIKA. 0:26"*)

Ext. Over London Streets – Christmas Morning.

(GHOST and SCROOGE 'fly'.)

GHOST OF CHRISTMAS PRESENT. Oh look dear! The snowy rooftops of old London town.

SCROOGE. *(eyes tight shut)* Agggghhh!

GHOST OF CHRISTMAS PRESENT. Like a Christmas card ain't it darlin'? *(hoity toity)* Get many cards this year dear? Hardly deluged I should imagine!
(laughs loudly) Ha ha ha ha! Ho ho ho ho!
(calls to the audience, tossing glitter) Merry Christmas! Merry Christmas everyone!

(If the audience wave back, SCROOGE doesn't see. His eyes are firmly shut as he clings on. They bounce into an air pocket.)

GHOST OF CHRISTMAS PRESENT. Whoops!

SCROOGE. *(clinging on)* Spirit!!!

GHOST OF CHRISTMAS PRESENT. Always a bit bumpy over Kentish Town. *(gasps)* But *LOOK* darlin'! Wait! Is it!? Yes! No! It IS! No! Is it?

(SCROOGE can bear it no more. Peeks one eye.)

SCROOGE. What!? What!??

GHOST OF CHRISTMAS PRESENT. Is that not your nephew's house dear?

SCROOGE. Nephew? Frederick? Which is Frederick's house?

GHOST OF CHRISTMAS PRESENT. The one with the lovely warm glow in the window dear. And the lovely twinklin' tree with all the presents under it. That one there dear.

(SCROOGE gazes intrigued. He tries to see where she's looking.)

No not that one there dear, this one 'ere dear. Ah! But then of course you would not know it darlin'. Never havin' been there. There again you have no wish to go

there do you darlin'? Invitin' you to Christmas once a
year! A blessed nuisance if ever there was one, ain't it
dear?

SCROOGE. It's intolerable!

GHOST OF CHRISTMAS PRESENT. Don't look at it dear.

SCROOGE. I won't!

GHOST OF CHRISTMAS PRESENT. Oh well alright then! Just
this once! If you insist. Just a tiny glimpse! Seein' as
it's Christmas!

SCROOGE. What!? No! I said – no! I don't want to go
there! I don't – what!!? NO!

(*The* **SPIRIT** *does her mystic gesture.* **SCROOGE** '*lands*'
heavily. [If the **ACTORS** *are carrying him, they could tip
him on to the stage, then pick him up and push him to
the window. Or allow him to hang there watching the
scene, just out of reach.]*)

(*Music: "LIEUTENANT KIJÉ: BURIAL OF KIJÉ.
1:00"** *)

---

* Please see Music Use Note, p. 3

Int. Frederick's House – Christmas Day.

(A comfortable, warm and welcoming feel. Christmas tree, presents, baubles and tinsel. The sound of little bells.)

*(Enter **FREDERICK** and his wife **CONSTANCE**. They are laughing.)*

CONSTANCE. Your turn now.

FREDERICK. My turn.

(He thinks.)

GHOST OF CHRISTMAS PRESENT. Who can that lovely lady be sir?

SCROOGE. No idea.

GHOST OF CHRISTMAS PRESENT. Course you do dear. That's Frederick's wife silly! Constance.

(Whacks his head, claps his ears, tweaks his nose.)

SCROOGE. Ow! Ow!! Ow!!!

GHOST OF CHRISTMAS PRESENT. But then you've never met her of course have you dear? My mistake dear. Sorry dear.

FREDERICK. Right. Got one.

CONSTANCE. Is he...a man?

FREDERICK. He is a man.

CONSTANCE. A young man?

FREDERICK. I wouldn't say a young man.

GHOST OF CHRISTMAS PRESENT. What on earth can they be talking about darlin'?

SCROOGE. They're playing a game.

GHOST OF CHRISTMAS PRESENT. What? A Christmas parlour game dear? Sorry – *(mimics **SCROOGE**)* – pathetic paltry Christmas parlour game dear?

SCROOGE. Who Am I?

GHOST OF CHRISTMAS PRESENT. *(looks at him)* Sorry dear?

SCROOGE. The name of the game is Who Am I? Something like that. I forget now.

GHOST OF CHRISTMAS PRESENT. Right.

CONSTANCE. A nice man?

FREDERICK. No. I wouldn't say – a nice man.

CONSTANCE. A nasty man then?

FREDERICK. You could say nasty.

CONSTANCE. How nasty? Really nasty?

FREDERICK. Really nasty!

CONSTANCE. Really *really* nasty?

FREDERICK. Really *really* nasty!

SCROOGE. *Who sir who!!!???*

CONSTANCE. Got it!

FREDERICK. Who then?

SCROOGE. *Who!!? Who!!?*

CONSTANCE. *Uncle Scrooge of course!*

FREDERICK. Uncle Scrooge! Uncle Scrooge!

SCROOGE. Me?

FREDERICK. Uncle Scrooge is coming to get you! Heh heh heh!!!!!!! Scroooge!! Scroooge!! Scroooge!!

(*Chases after her making Scroogy noises.*)

CONSTANCE. Fred! Fred!! You'll frighten the children!

(*They run round laughing. He catches her. They kiss.*)

SCROOGE. Well I'm glad! Glad I frighten children! Children *should* be frightened! *All children should be frightened!*

GHOST OF CHRISTMAS PRESENT. Thank you for that pearl of parental wisdom dear. And whenever you're ready darlin'!

(**GHOST** *pulls* **SCROOGE.**)

SCROOGE. No! What!? Wait! *WAAAAIT!!*

GHOST OF CHRISTMAS PRESENT. Can't 'ang about darlin'!

(*They 'take off' again.*)

SCROOGE. Aggghhh! Nooooo!

GHOST OF CHRISTMAS PRESENT. 'Cos now to other Christmases must we go. And not all so sweet as them was sadly. To the poor parts of London sir. You've heard of the poor parts?

SCROOGE. I have heard of 'em. Little point in seeing 'em.

GHOST OF CHRISTMAS PRESENT. Though you'd hardly think these ones poor, they done it up so nice. With so little sir.

SCROOGE. Who? Who have?

GHOST OF CHRISTMAS PRESENT. *(Waves her hands. Mystic gesture.)* Behold sir if you would sir, please sir.

Int. Cratchit's House – Christmas Day.

(**ACTORS 2** and 5 *enter. They run round, bringing on basic pieces of set for the Cratchit scene: table, chairs, door. [They might also play the furniture – as in the Counting House.])*

(*They also play the* **CRATCHIT CHILDREN***: **KATIE**, **ABIGAIL**, **URSULA** and **PETER**.)*

(**SCROOGE** *watches the ensuing scene. The* **GHOST** *watches too, sometimes standing beside him, sometimes not. She occasionally plays* **MARTHA***, the eldest Cratchit.)*

(**ACTOR 4** *enters as* **MRS. CRATCHIT***.)*

MRS. CRATCHIT. *(calls off)* Katie! Abigail! Are you putting on your ribbons and your clean smocks?

KATIE AND ABIGAIL. *(call out)* Yes mother.

(**MRS. CRATCHIT** *weaves in and out of* **ACTORS 2** *and* 5 *as they assemble or mime the Cratchit set.)*

MRS. CRATCHIT. Lay this table be a dear Peter.

PETER CRATCHIT. Righto mother.

MRS. CRATCHIT. *(calls off)* Ursula?

URSULA. *(calls out)* Yes mother?

MRS. CRATCHIT. Gravy browning?

URSULA. Tasty as anything mother.

MRS. CRATCHIT. *(calls off)* How's the turkey Martha?

GHOST OF CHRISTMAS PRESENT. *(as* **MARTHA***)* Sizzling lovely mother.

(**SCROOGE** *double-takes on the* **GHOST** *doing* **MARTHA***'s voice.)*

MRS. CRATCHIT. Katie! Abigail! Are you ready?

KATIE AND ABIGAIL. *(call out)* Coming mother!

SCROOGE. Who are these wretched people?

MRS. CRATCHIT. Oh heavens! Whatever's got Mr. Cratchit then?

SCROOGE. Cratchit!?

GHOST OF CHRISTMAS PRESENT. That's right dear.

SCROOGE. *Cratchit's house!?*

MRS. CRATCHIT. And Tiny Tim's with him. Where *can* they be?

PETER CRATCHIT. They'll be here in a jiff mother.

GHOST OF CHRISTMAS PRESENT. *(as* **MARTHA***)* Fret not mother.

*(***SCROOGE** *double-takes again.)*

SCROOGE. Tiny what!?

GHOST OF CHRISTMAS PRESENT. Tim dear.

MRS. CRATCHIT. Katie! Abigail! There you are!

*(***ACTORS 2 AND 5** *run in as* **KATIE** *and* **ABIGAIL***. They run round giggling.)*

Now help your sister Martha!

KATIE/ABIGAIL. Yes mother.

MRS. CRATCHIT. Everything ready Peter?

PETER CRATCHIT. All ready mother.

*(***MRS. CRATCHIT** *and* **ACTORS 2** *and* **5** *run round each other, getting ready for Christmas dinner. They appear to run through* **SCROOGE***.* **ACTOR 2** *exits.* **SCROOGE** *jumps out of the way with a shriek.)*

SCROOGE. Aggghh!

GHOST OF CHRISTMAS PRESENT. They cannot see you dear. As we been explainin'. They are in another molecular dimension as it is known. *(Einstein)* Or rather vill be known.

SCROOGE. What!?

GHOST OF CHRISTMAS PRESENT. *(Cockney)* Don't ask darlin'!

MRS. CRATCHIT. *(looking through window)* Look Look children! Here they come now! Father! And Tiny Tim!

ACTOR 5 AND GHOST. It's father, father! Father and Tiny Tim!

(BOB CRATCHIT enters with TINY TIM on his shoulder. TINY TIM is a lame and sickly seven year-old. He could be mimed, a puppet, a mask or simply a voice.)

BOB CRATCHIT. Happy Christmas my beloved ones!

MRS. CRATCHIT. Blessings be Mr. Cratchit! *(suddenly anxious)* And how did Tiny Tim fare?

BOB CRATCHIT. How did you fare Tiny Tim?

TINY TIM. As good as gold as I hope mother!

MRS. CRATCHIT AND CHILDREN. Good Tiny Tim, good!

TINY TIM. And now I'm ready for my dinner.

(Everyone claps. TINY TIM claps too. CRATCHIT lifts him to the ground. TINY TIM walks firmly but painfully towards the table. SCROOGE gazes wide-eyed.)

(Music: "IN THE BLEAK MIDWINTER" – Ketil Bjornstad – The Rainbow Sessions. 0:45*)

(They all watch with baited breath until TINY TIM sits at last in his seat. Audible relief as he does so.)

MRS. CRATCHIT. *(She kisses him.)* Ah my blessed boy! But – *(Under her breath)* – how was he?

CRATCHIT. Strong and hearty as the best of 'em my dear Mrs. C.

(A painful moment. They know this isn't true. CRATCHIT claps his hands.)

Now then my dearest ones! Where is our Christmas feast we heard so much about, eh Tiny Tim?

MRS. CRATCHIT. What did you hear father?

CRATCHIT. Well that our turkey is a mighty feathered phenomenon. The greatest turkey ever known! That Ursula's gravy is hissing hot and Master Peter's potatoes mashed to a tee and Miss Kate and Miss Abigail's apple-sauce the sweetest this side of China and Miss Martha's chestnut stuffing fit for no less than our beloved queen herself!

---

*Please see Music Use Note, p. 3

(MRS. CRATCHIT exits. Returns with the turkey. It is tiny. Even SCROOGE looks twice.)

MRS. CRATCHIT. Ta-da!

TINY TIM. Ta-da!

CRATCHIT AND CHILDREN. Hooray!!!

(She puts it on the table. MR. CRATCHIT carves. MRS. CRATCHIT serves.)

(Music: "THE HOLLY AND THE IVY" – 'Celtic Tidings' – Chris Caswell)

GHOST OF CHRISTMAS PRESENT. Well darlin'? This is a 'profligate Christmas bean-feast' to be sure!

SCROOGE. Profligate. Precisely.

GHOST OF CHRISTMAS PRESENT. All 'humbug' ain't it sir?

SCROOGE. Humbug! Exactly!

GHOST OF CHRISTMAS YET TO COME. A sham and a fraud sir!

SCROOGE. A sham and a fraud indeed!

CRATCHIT. But first a toast! To Mrs. Cratchit and all my blessed Cratchits! Merry Christmas to us, my dears. And God bless us all!

TINY TIM. God bless us each and all and every one!

(Everyone claps, except SCROOGE. CRATCHIT holds TINY TIM close, holds his hand in his. MRS. CRATCHIT wipes away a tear. The CRATCHITS tuck into their tiny turkey. SCROOGE gazes at the scene.)

SCROOGE. This um – this – er – child?

GHOST OF CHRISTMAS PRESENT. Tiny Tim darlin'?

SCROOGE. Tiny – um – whatever, yes.

GHOST OF CHRISTMAS PAST. What of him dear?

SCROOGE. Will he – will they –

GHOST OF CHRISTMAS PRESENT. – put him somewhere dear? 'Are there no workhouses'? 'No prisons' they could bung him in? Or up a chimney p'raps? Or down a coal mine? All on his own dear? In the dark

dear? Children is highly prized in mines so I hear,
'Cos the mines is so narrow and twisty-like. Or – better
if he died. Do us all a favour. Wouldn't yer say darlin'?

SCROOGE. So will he?

GHOST OF CHRISTMAS PRESENT. What dear?

SCROOGE. Die?

GHOST OF CHRISTMAS PRESENT. I am but the spirit of
Christmas Present, sir. I live but for a day. I cannot
tell thee dear. Sorry.

SCROOGE. Simply – simply I mean simply that if he
should – er – die, it will grieve Cratchit presumably
so it will make his work that much slower. Which will
impact upon the exigencies and necessities of my
business. Which is the reason I ask it obviously.

GHOST OF CHRISTMAS PRESENT. But it would 'decrease the
surplus population'? Would it not sir?

SCROOGE. It would. Precisely.

GHOST OF CHRISTMAS PRESENT. 'Boo hoo hoo but there
we are'. Ain't that how it goes sir?

SCROOGE. Indeed it is madam.

TINY TIM. Tell us a story father?

CRATCHIT. After supper Tiny Tim.

TINY TIM. Will you tell us my favourite? Ali Baba and the
Forty Thieves?

SCROOGE. *(starts)* Ali Baba?

TINY TIM. When he finds the hidden treasure in the deep
dark cave? Oh please father. When he says 'Open
Sesame!'

SCROOGE. Open Sesame?

(**GHOST** *watches* **SCROOGE** *as the memory stirs.*)

TINY TIM. And finds the rubies and the diamonds and the
bright blue sapphires? Oh please father please!

CRATCHIT. *(hugs* **TINY TIM***)* I will tell it to us all little man,
but first let us sing I do declare!

(**CRATCHIT, MRS. CRATCHIT** *and* **TINY TIM** *join in with 'THE HOLLY AND THE IVY'.*)

(**SCROOGE** *watches them sing. Suddenly he can take it no more.*)

SCROOGE. Cratchit!! CRATCHIT!! Stop it! Stop it!!! What are you thinking of man! All this – this – frittering away money you do not even have on such pointless trivial Christmas – jollities!

(*The* **CRATCHITS** *sing on, oblivious.*)

All this potatoes and – chestnut stuffing and – and cranberry sauce and – brussel sprouts and – and gravy and – and – CRATCHIT! The money, Cratchit! Stop this! We need to count the money! Now! On the dot Cratchit! It can't wait Cratchit! *UNLOCK THE BOX AND DO THE AUDIT CRATCHIT! CRATCHIT!*

GHOST OF CHRISTMAS PRESENT. Sir?

SCROOGE. *CRATCHIT! I NEED YOU CRATCHIT!!*

GHOST OF CHRISTMAS PRESENT. He cannot hear thee sir.

SCROOGE. Yes yes!

GHOST OF CHRISTMAS PRESENT. We're in a different molecular –

SCROOGE. Yes I know that! I'm quite cognizent of that thank you!

GHOST OF CHRISTMAS PRESENT. Now we must leave this vision sir.

(**GHOST** *waves her hands. The singing* **CRATCHITS** *fade.*)

SCROOGE. Good! Good riddance to it spirit! Good riddance to all of you Cratchits!

(**GHOST** *makes her mystic gesture.* **SCROOGE** *and the* **GHOST** *"fly."* **SCROOGE** *shrieks again but getting used to it.*)

SCROOGE. Agggh!! Right. Now then, if you'd kindly convey me to my home thank you, we can all –

(Sound Effect: Enormous crowd gathered. Sounds of children.)

SCROOGE. Now what!? What is that? That fiendish noise!?

GHOST OF CHRISTMAS PRESENT. More that you have not seen sir.

SCROOGE. *(Looks down. Strains his eyes to see.)* What? What are all these – (*GASPS as he looks down*) Where are we!?

Ext. Kennington Common, London – Christmas Day.

GHOST OF CHRISTMAS PRESENT. Kennington Common dear.

SCROOGE. Kennington Common!?? Kennington – *(GASPS again)* There's thousands! Thousands and thousands of – *(nearly falls) Agggh!* Look at them all! *WHO ARE THEY!?*

GHOST OF CHRISTMAS PRESENT. Just the homeless, that's all it is darlin'. Them as 'as nothin' sir. No work, no homes, just 'emselves sir. From all over Britain they've come. To seek the rights that is theirs sir.

SCROOGE. *(shouts down at the crowd)* Layabouts! Criminals! Vagabonds! Who do they think they are?

GHOST OF CHRISTMAS PRESENT. The People – is who they are dear. Not layabouts or criminals or vagabonds. Or wastrels as Parliament and the newspapers would have us believe. But orderly and sober and peaceable sir. Singin' at the city gates. 'Til they're heard darlin'.

SCROOGE. *(covering his ears)* Well I can't hear them!

GHOST OF CHRISTMAS PRESENT. *(pulls his hands from his ears) LISTEN SIR!*

SCROOGE. *OW!!!*

> (ACTORS 2, 4, *and* 5 *are the* **PEOPLE OF ENGLAND.**
> **ACTOR 5** *begins to sing.)*

> (Music: "HARD TIMES OF OLD ENGLAND" TRAD)

ACTOR 5. *(sings)*
> OH PEOPLE OF ENGLAND I'LL SING YOU A SONG,
> OUR HOMES ARE NO MORE AND THE WORK IS ALL GONE,
> THE RICH HAVE IT ALL, THE POOR MAN HAS NONE. AND
> IT'S –

ALL. *(sing)*
> OH, THE HARD TIMES OF OLD ENGLAND,
> IN OLD ENGLAND VERY HARD TIMES.

ACTORS 2 AND 4. *(sing)*
> SO TAKE TO THE ROAD, IT'S THE LIFE THAT WE CHOOSE,

WE MAY NOT HAVE SHELTER, NOT EVEN HAVE SHOES,
BUT WHEN YOU'VE GOT NOTHING, YOU'VE NOTHING
  TO LOSE.

(Sound: Huge crowd sing chorus, comes in with the **ACTORS***:)*

ALL. *(sing)*
AND IT'S –
OH, THE HARD TIMES OF OLD ENGLAND,
IN OLD ENGLAND VERY HARD TIMES.
WE SAY OH, THE HARD TIMES OF OLD ENGLAND,
IN OLD ENGLAND VERY HARD TIMES.

SCROOGE. They should listen to the people governing, that's what the 'People' should do!

GHOST OF CHRISTMAS PRESENT. I'd say their faith in the people governin' i.e. the Government is on the whole infinitesimal sir. Whilst their faith in the people bein' governed – i.e. themselves – i.e. the People sir – is on the whole illimitable sir.

SCROOGE. 'The People'!? 'The People'!? This is about *me* isn't it? This journey you've forced me on! Not about 'The People'! About *me!!*

GHOST OF CHRISTMAS PRESENT. Quite right darlin'! My mistake. Sorry! All about you darlin'. But – *(sees something)* – well! That's a coincidence!

(Sound: Cuts abruptly)

SCROOGE. What?

GHOST OF CHRISTMAS PRESENT. 'Cos 'ere is more about you sir, right 'ere sir. Wouldya credit it sir!?

(Music: "COVENTRY CAROL" fades up)

SCROOGE. Stop that! Stop that racket! Turn it off!

*(***ACTORS*** bring on Frederick's House. A Christmas tree arrives.* **SCROOGE** *watches aghast as he recognizes the set.)*

What's this? Wait a minute! No No! We've done this! We've been here already! Spirit!!

(The **GHOST** *conducts the singing.)*

GHOST OF CHRISTMAS PRESENT. Pardon dear?

(Music: CAROL builds)

SCROOGE. Stop that! Stop that noise! *(covering his ears)* Turn it off this moment!

(The **ACTORS** *continue to create Frederick's House. Presents, baubles and tinsel. The* **GHOST** *conducts away.)*

(Music: CAROL louder)

*(***SCROOGE** *shouts in terror at the* **GHOST** *and the* **ACTORS**.*)*

SCROOGE. *STOP IT I SAY!! STOP IT!! TURN IT OFF!!! QUIET! GO AWAY!!! ALL OF YOU!!! GET RID OF IT!!!*

GHOST OF CHRISTMAS PRESENT. Sorry sir.

(Music: CAROL cuts)

(Lights change.)

Int. Frederick's House – Christmas Day.

(Frederick's house in place, exactly as it was. **FREDERICK**
and **CONSTANCE** *in place, exactly as they were. The
sound of little bells.)*

SCROOGE. No no no!!! Did you not hear me spirit!!?
We've had this scene! We don't need to do it again!!
We know what happens! I said did you not hear me
madam!!!!

GHOST OF CHRISTMAS PRESENT. Certainly did darlin'.

(She makes a mystic gesture. **FREDERICK** *and*
CONSTANCE *spring into action.)*

FREDERICK. Uncle Scroooge is coming to get you! Heh
heh heh!!!! Scrooooge!! Scrooooge!! Scrooooge!!

SCROOGE. *(shouts at* **FREDERICK** *and* **CONSTANCE***)* Stop it!
Stop it! Stop it!

CONSTANCE. Fred! Fred! Fred!! You'll frighten the
children!

(They run round laughing. He catches her. They kiss.
SCROOGE *watches aghast.)*

SCROOGE. Off! D'ye hear me! We've done this bit! *TURN
IT OFF!!*

GHOST OF CHRISTMAS PRESENT. Not all of it sir.

CONSTANCE. You can keep your uncle Scrooge! I have no
patience with him.

SCROOGE. *Away with them spirit!*

FREDERICK. Well I am sorry for him.

*(***SCROOGE** *freezes.)*

CONSTANCE. Sorry for him!??

FREDERICK. And I will invite him and I will keep inviting
him.

CONSTANCE. *(kisses him)* Perhaps you see your mother in
him darling Freddy.

FREDERICK. Perhaps I do. I may hate what he does, all the misery he brings, but – I cannot hate *him*. I should. I know I *should*. But I – cannot. And – *(remembers)* – yes!

CONSTANCE. What?

FREDERICK. Something –

CONSTANCE. What?

FREDERICK. – well – shook him yesterday. When we spoke. We spoke of – love.

CONSTANCE. Love? Scrooge spoke of love?

FREDERICK. He railed at our marriage.

CONSTANCE. Of course!

FREDERICK. But there was something else.

(Music: "SIXTH SENSE – Mind Reading"*)

Something else there. I saw it.

CONSTANCE. What?

FREDERICK. For a moment only. In his face. A sudden haunting.

SCROOGE. Enough Spirit!

GHOST OF CHRISTMAS PRESENT. Quiet darlin' please!

FREDERICK. Made me think. Love and the not getting of it –

SCROOGE. *SPIRIT!*

FREDERICK. – is bad enough. But love and the not *giving* of it can lock up a man's soul for eternity.

*(**CONSTANCE** kisses **FREDERICK** with the greatest tenderness. **SCROOGE** watches frozen, unspeaking.)*

(Music: "LIEUTENANT KIJÉ: TROIKA. 0:25"**)

(Sound: Happy jangling of door bells. Whoops and greetings, Merry Christmases, children laughing, boots stamped.)

---

*Please see Music Use Note, p. 3
**Please see Music Use Note, p. 3

(CONSTANCE and FREDERICK run off. They take the pieces of set with them. They appear to run through SCROOGE. SCROOGE spins round, spins back furiously. Watches as they vanish. He and the GHOST are left alone on the bare stage.)

SCROOGE. *NO MADAM!!!!*

(Music and Sound: Cut)

We did not speak of love! Love was *not* spoken of! I do *NOT* speak of love madam! It is not a thing I speak of! Love! Love! Ha! I see your game madam! You make it all up! That's what you do! All this past and present nonsense! Just cheap *MAGIC TRICKS!* Mere chicanery madam! Skullduggery! That's all it is! To make me think I see what I do not! Well I am not a gawping gullible fool like Jacob Marley!

(mimics MARLEY) Oooh! Ooooh! Repent! Repent! Change thine ways! Beg forgiveness old friend! No madam!! I am Ebenezer Scrooge! And repenting and relenting and *CHANGING* is not what Ebenezer Scrooge does! Beg forgiveness! LOVE! No madam! Scrooges don't beg forgiveness and –

(The SPIRIT listens calmly. SCROOGE rants away.)

– Scrooges don't love! It is not in our natures to LOVE madam! Not in my nature! Not in my father's nature! Not in any of our natures! D'ye hear me ghost?!!? *LOVE!!??* Love is *HUMBUG!!!*

GHOST OF CHRISTMAS PRESENT. *(looking into his face)* What are these dear?

SCROOGE. What?

GHOST OF CHRISTMAS PRESENT. Tears darlin'?

SCROOGE. *TEARS!!??*

(wipes them away furiously) Ridiculous!! Ha! Men do not have tears! Tears are aberrant to a man's nature. They are women's things. Because women cry. And women are not to be trusted.

GHOST OF CHRISTMAS PRESENT. Why sir?

SCROOGE. Because women *LEAVE* madam!!!!

GHOST OF CHRISTMAS PRESENT. I am sorry for thee sir.

SCROOGE. No I am sorry for thee spirit! You've had a wasted night. You and your colleague. Colleaguesss! You are done and I have won madam! Now if you'd kindly convey me back to my office. Tomorrow is my *counting day! My yearly audit!* When all sums are accounted for, all debts paid and all books balanced! I hope you don't charge for your ghosting by the way! If so you'd be making a massive *LOSS! (laughs uproariously)* Ha ha ha ha! So spirit if you'd kindly –

(He looks round for her.)

– spirit?

(The **SPIRIT** *is nowhere to be seen.)*

Spirit!?

(He runs round the stage.)

Spirit!

(He shouts into the audience.)

SPIRIT!!!

(Lights change. **ACTORS 3, 4,** *and* **5** *set up or become Scrooge's Counting House.)*

(Sound Effect: London street sounds. Horses hooves, barrel organ.)

Int. Scrooge's Counting House. Night.

(**SCROOGE** *staggers, spins around. Recognises his Counting House.*)

SCROOGE. Ah! Well. Thank you spirit! You finally got the point. I'm back! As I requested. No broken bones. Everything – *(sees the* **ACTORS***)* Ah! Everything as we were. Splendid! My little Counting House – *(surprised)* – very neat and tidy but otherwise the same. Cratchit must have had a tidy up. Well done Cratchit! Everything tickety-boo! As it tickety should be! *(chuckles loudly)* Don't expect a raise Cratchit. *(Chuckles louder. Looks through window.)* No sign outside. Strange. Mmmm. Fog coming down.

(Fog drifts beyond the window.)

Good old London fog. The world as it was. Me as I was. My money as it – *(freezes)* My money!!!

(He shoots off to get his money, reaching into his waistcoat pocket for the key. He freezes mid-stage. GASPS as he realises he's not wearing his waistcoat.)

Agggh! Nightgown! What am I doing in my nightgown? No key! Where's the key!? My key!!! *KEY!!! CRATCHIT!!!!!*

(Music: "BARBASTELLA – BATMAN BEGINS" soundtrack*)

(The fog creeps through the door, across the stage, prowls into the Counting House.)

(The **GHOST OF CHRISTMAS YET TO COME** *appears behind Scrooge. It begins to grow ominously and inexorably behind him.* **SCROOGE** *spins round, sees the* **GHOST** *in the looming fog. He gasps in terror.)*

Aggggghh! (calms down) Ah! First customer. Splendid. Charmed I'm sure. Charmant charmant! Enchantée! As the French would say. Or parlez. *(He laughs urbanely.)* Do sit down why don't you?

---

*Please see Music Use Note, p. 3

(The **GHOST** *doesn't move.)*

Very well stand if you wish. So – how may we assist? A little – loan perhaps?

(The **GHOST** *doesn't move.)*

Oh! A larger loan possibly? A VAST loan no less! Excellent suggestion! *(chortles merrily)* Oh sorry! *(looks round for the phonograph)* Where's the – er – normally we – er – Cratchit! Anyway – um –

(Mimes winding it up. Mimics a tinny carol.) 'We wish you a merry Christmas, we wish you a merry – um –' Anyway – ha ha! Do beg pardon. *(proffers hand)* Don't think we've been –

GHOST OF CHRISTMAS YET TO COME. I am the third spirit. The Ghost of Christmas Yet To Come sir.

(Sound Effect: Cock crows)

SCROOGE. Ah no no no! Clearly the message never reached you. I told her! You know, the last one! Her! I am beyond spirits. I have no further spirit-ual requirement thank you!

*(***SCROOGE** *chuckles. The* **GHOST** *doesn't move.)*

Thank you!

(The **GHOST** *doesn't move.)*

Besides it is not Christmas yet to come! It is *this* Christmas, the one we are *in* sir! Everything as it was, everything as it should be and everything as it – as it – jolly well will be! Hah! All I need is the *KEY!*

GHOST OF CHRISTMAS YET TO COME. Key to what sir?

SCROOGE. *To my money sir! Idiot!*

GHOST OF CHRISTMAS YET TO COME. The money is gone sir.

*(***SCROOGE** *freezes.)*

SCROOGE. Sorry?

GHOST OF CHRISTMAS YET TO COME. Gone sir.

SCROOGE. Gone? *Gone!!!? GONE!!!!!???*

(He charges offstage. A terrible scream.)

AGGGGGHHHHH!!!!

(He charges back. The **GHOST** *is growing.)*

Where is it! My box!!! MY BOX!!! *WHO'S TAKEN IT SPIRIT!!!??*

GHOST OF CHRISTMAS YET TO COME. The Queen sir.

SCROOGE. The Queen? What she doing with it!?

GHOST OF CHRISTMAS YET TO COME. Her Majesty's Treasury sir. They own it now.

(The **GHOST** *is growing.)*

(Music: Builds)

SCROOGE. Own it!? OWN IT!? That is not possible! Unless – unless I was dead sir! Which obviously I'm not sir!

(He laughs uproariously.) Ha ha ha ha ha! *(stops laughing)* Wait! WAIT! *(Truth dawns.)* I know what you're up to spirit. You have hidden my money to make me *think* I'm dead! That I am deceased! And that I lie at this moment frozen, lifeless and alone in some dark, deep, dank, dolorous grave sir to make me – ha ha ha ha ha! – repent sir! To make me change sir! Ha ha ha ha ha! Well, as I've said many many times sir, I won't repent sir! And I won't CHANGE sir! Not ever sir! Ha ha ha ha ha! So give me back my money sir if you would please! Spirit of Christmas Yet To Come! D'ye hear me sir!!??

*(***SCROOGE*** dances about, shouting up at the ever-growing* **GHOST***.)*

I said d'you hear me sir!!!???

(The **GHOST***'s eyes start glowing red.)*

SCROOGE. No no no sir!! You won't frighten me sir! Just my money if you please sir!? My money!!!! And be quick about it! *I COMMAND IT SIR!!!*

(The **GHOST** *is now enormous, his eyes gleaming redder and redder.)*

Right! Have it your own way. I know who'll help me!

*(***SCROOGE*** runs up to the* **ACTORS** *in the same positions as in Scene One. He jumps up and down and shouts.)*

SCROOGE. Where is it!!? You know where it is!! *Where's my money!!!*

(The **ACTORS** *do not react or obey. They stare implacably back.)*

(The **GHOST** *fills the stage. His glowing red eyes dazzle* **SCROOGE.** **SCROOGE** *hollers at the* **GHOST** *and the* **ACTORS.***)*

SCROOGE. *MY MONEY!!!! GIVE ME MY MONEY!!!!!!*

(Music: Cuts)

(Sound Effect: Keys at the door)

(The door opens. **CRATCHIT** *enters.)*

Ah Cratchit! Thank God thank God! Just in time Cratchit!

*(***CRATCHIT*** walks straight past* **SCROOGE.***)*

Ah! You see spirit? He'll have hidden the box away for safekeeping. That's what's happened. A slightly more likely explanation than yours I think spirit! So all is well. Ha! Cratchit? Cratchit?

*(***CRATCHIT*** looks at his key chain, chooses a key.)*

The key! Ha! Look! He has the key! Cratchit? Cratchit! There appears to have been a slight mistake. If you'd kindly show this – er – dark – er – gentleman that my money's safe and all is well? Cratchit? Cratchit!

*(***CRATCHIT*** ignores him. Goes to a tiny single drawer. Unlocks it.)*

No not in there Cratchit! My money's not in there! It wouldn't fit! Ha! Show him the box Cratchit! Cratchit!

Why won't you answer me!? What's the matter with you Cratchit? *CRATCHIT!!*

GHOST OF CHRISTMAS YET TO COME. His mind is on other things sir.

(CRATCHIT opens the drawer.)

SCROOGE. Other things? There are no other things! *Where's the box Cratchit!*

(CRATCHIT takes out a cardboard box. He holds it with great tenderness.)

No! That's not the box! No!! –

(CRATCHIT gently opens the box. Takes out something wrapped in brown paper.)

What are you doing Cratchit!!? What's this?

(CRATCHIT carefully unwraps the brown paper and there is the leather-bound story book from the school room. Faded and battered and still in two pieces but otherwise intact. CRATCHIT gazes at the book as the mist gathers around it. SCROOGE gasps.)

My book!

CRATCHIT. *(looks up, calls to the flies)* Tiny Tim? If you can hear me where you are. Since your passing.

SCROOGE. Passing? Tiny Tim?

CRATCHIT. I would bring thee comfort sir, wherever you dwell. I hope in a place of peace. But perhaps it is to seek peace for myself. For you are my light in the darkness little man. Please may I read to you as I used to? Only *I* knew where this was. He'd forgotten all about it. His book of treasures.

SCROOGE. Treasures.

CRATCHIT. I learnt the stories off by heart. I know 'em all now. Every one of 'em. Worth more than all the money ever made, Mr. Scrooge sir. It is your heart you see sir. Even you had a heart would you believe Mr. Scrooge?

(**SCROOGE** *tries to reply but cannot. He watches spellbound.*)

Even in two bits and all battered and locked away in a cupboard. But you kept it sir. Even though you didn't know you did sir. Even though you forgot it was even there sir. Some part of you, some tiny beating part of you, could not bear to lose it. And that makes all the difference. You kept it old Scrooge! Doesn't that bring hope to the whole rolling world sir? That a Scrooge can love stories? That a Scrooge can have a heart? Even though he doesn't know it? Doesn't it, Tiny Tim? My dear one. *(He looks up.)* What shall we read? *(He turns the pages.)* I know. How about – your favourite?

SCROOGE. *(whispers)* Ali Baba.

CRATCHIT. Ali Baba. And the Cave of Treasures. And so I will Tiny Tim. But we always like reading this bit first don't we?

(**SCROOGE** *stretches his hand and opens the book simultaneously with* **CRATCHIT**. *Very tenderly, they reveal the title page.*)

(reads) "This book is for you my sweet darling boy. A book of treasures to guide your life. And if I –"

(**SCROOGE'S MOTHER** *appears from the shadows.*)

SCROOGE'S MOTHER. – cannot remain with thee as the doctors tell me I must not, then know how very dearly I would do if I could, and how very nearly did I see this one Christmas with you – your first ever Christmas – that I know now I will not. How many many Christmases would I spend with you if I could. Just one more hour of life with you would be the dearest gift, no earthly riches could compare. But since I cannot, know that I will look over you and will love you always as I always did from the first sweet breath you drew. And do so now and always will forever. And forever. With my eternal blessing. Your mother. Seventeen hundred and seventy-seven. Christmas.

*(**SCROOGE** is overcome with emotion. Real tears fall. The **GHOST** watches.)*

CRATCHIT. So you was loved Mr. Scrooge. All that time. Who'd a' thought it? Even though you never knew 'er sir. She loved you Mr Scrooge. And you loved her, didn't yer sir? Like all the Cratchits love Mrs. Cratchit! Didn't you sir?

SCROOGE. *(barely audible)* I did. I do.

*(Suddenly a **VOICE** shatters the moment. The shadow of the **GHOST** morphs into the giant figure of **GRIMES** the school master.)*

GRIMES. SCROOGE*!!*

*(**SCROOGE** freezes. Gazes up at him.)*

What's this!!? Robin Hood! Robinson Crusoe! Jack the Giant Killer! *ALI BABA!!? OPEN SESAME!!? STORIES BOY!!? PALTRY POINTLESS STORIES!??*

(raises his cane) FAIRY TALES!!? Give me the book boy! Vile witless pointless boy! Give it to me!!! Scrooge!!! GIVE!!! SCROOGE!!!

SCROOGE. Yes sir.

GRIMES. That's right boy. Quickly boy quickly! I'm waitin' Scrooge! I'm waitin'!

*(**SCROOGE** looks up at **GRIMES**.)*

SCROOGE. No sir.

GRIMES. What!!? What was that!?? Whatcher say boy!? *SCROOGE!!!!!!!?*

SCROOGE. I said no sir. It is my book sir. It is my most special treasure. Given to me by someone I loved. Yes, loved sir. And you're not to have it. Not ever. No-one is to have it. Except Tiny Tim. And Bob Cratchit actually. And all the Cratchits actually. And all the children of all the world actually if you want to know sir actually. *SO MR. GRIMES SIR – (He takes a deep breath.) GET THEE GONE SIR!*

(**GRIMES** *ROARS. He lifts his cane.* **SCROOGE** *does not flinch.* **GRIMES** *freezes mid-stroke. He tries to shout, tries to scream, but cannot.* **SCROOGE** *faces him, 'til* **GRIMES** *slowly inevitably dissolves.* **SCROOGE'S MOTHER** *sings the "Coventry Carol".*)

SCROOGE'S MOTHER.
LULLY, LULLAY, THOU LITTLE TINY CHILD,
BY, BY, LULLY, LULLAY.
LULLAY, THOU LITTLE TINY CHILD.
BY, BY, LULLY, LULLAY.

(**SCROOGE** *joins her softly. They sing the carol together.*)

SCROOGE AND MOTHER.
LULLAY TOO, HOW MAY WE DO
FOR TO PRESERVE THIS DAY
THIS POOR YOUNGLING
FOR WHOM WE DO SING
BY, BY, LULLY, LULLAY.

(*The carol ends.* **SCROOGE'S MOTHER** *fades.*)

(**SCROOGE** *alone with* **CRATCHIT**. *The* **GHOST OF CHRISTMAS YET TO COME** *reappears.*)

GHOST OF CHRISTMAS YET TO COME. Sir?

SCROOGE. Yes?

GHOST OF CHRISTMAS YET TO COME. We must leave now sir.

SCROOGE. Sorry?

GHOST OF CHRISTMAS YET TO COME. Leave sir.

SCROOGE. Leave?

GHOST OF CHRISTMAS YET TO COME. 'Tis the end sir.

SCROOGE. The end? End of what?

GHOST OF CHRISTMAS YET TO COME. Of the play sir.

SCROOGE. The play!? What play!?

GHOST OF CHRISTMAS YET TO COME. This play.

ACTOR 2. The one you're in.

SCROOGE. What!? Cratchit!!? What are you doing!? I'm not in a play!

*(Enter three other **ACTORS**.)*

ACTOR 3. Yes you are. What do you think this is? *(pointing at stage, pointing at audience)*

ACTOR 4. What do you think they're doing?

SCROOGE. Who?

ACTOR 3. Them.

> **(SCROOGE** *sees the audience for the first time. Double takes, staggers with shock.)*

SCROOGE. But – but –

ACTOR 4. But it's ended now. Because you're dead. Sadly for you.

*(The **GHOST** reveals a scythe. **SCROOGE** gasps.)*

GHOST OF CHRISTMAS YET TO COME. Sorry.

SCROOGE. Dead!!?

ACTOR 3. Good for us though 'Cos we get off early.

ACTORS. Yay!!!

SCROOGE. No I'm not!

ACTOR 2. Afraid you are.

SCROOGE. No!!!

GHOST OF CHRISTMAS YET TO COME. After you Scrooge.

*(The **GHOST** vanishes. Lights change.)*

SCROOGE. DEAD!! No no no no!! I can't be! I can't be!

*(The **ACTORS** cheerfully remove the set. They chat to **SCROOGE** as they do so.)*

ACTOR 3. Gave you enough clues! Office all clean and empty.

ACTOR 2. No Scrooge and Marley sign. No box of money.

ACTOR 4. All gone.

ACTOR 3. No more Scrooge.

ACTOR 2. Caput!

ACTOR 4. Finito!

ACTOR 3. Shuffled off thy mortal coil!

SCROOGE. Shuffled off my –

ACTOR 4. Dead as a doornail.

SCROOGE. Dead as a – no!! –

ACTOR 2. *(as* **MARLEY***)* Can't get much deader than that Ebenezer.

*(***ACTOR 5** *enters.)*

ACTOR 5. The faceless executioner comes to us all in his time, doth he not Mr. Scrooge?

(The **ACTORS** *hastily clear the stage.* **SCROOGE** *tries to stop them. The words tumble out as he runs frantically from one to the other.)*

SCROOGE. No no no no wait! Wait!! Stop stop! I don't want to die! It's too soon! I'll – I'll repent! I will! I – I – I – promise! I'll – I'll – honour Christmas in my heart and keep it all the year. I shall live in the past and the present and the future. And not forget the lessons of each. The past to learn from and – and let go.

ACTORS. *(linking hands)* Scrooge!

SCROOGE. *(gabbling even faster)* The – the – future not to fret about that which I can do nothing, the present to learn to live – to live – each blessed living – moment! *(calls up into the flies)* Spirits! Help me!

ACTOR 3. We are the spirits.

(as the **GHOST OF CHRISTMAS PRESENT***)* That was us darlin'! *Ooooh Scrooooooge!*

ACTORS 2,4,5. *(as* **MARLEY, GHOST OF CHRISTMAS PAST, GHOST OF CHRISTMAS YET TO COME***) Ooooh Scrooooooge!*

SCROOGE. WAIT!! NO! NO! I beg of you! I swear – I swear – I swear – I swear – I've – I've – I've – I've – *CHANGED!!!*

(The **ACTORS** *stop. Look at* **SCROOGE***.)*

(Music: "MISS HAVERSHAM" – 'GREAT EXPECTATIONS (2014)' soundtrack*)

ACTOR 5. Changed?

SCROOGE. *(He really means it.)* Yes! Yes! Yes! Changed! Changed! I have! I have! I've changed! I've changed!

(falls to his knees)

I have! I have! I really really really have!

(pause)

I have!

(The **ACTORS** *look at each other. They consider. They decide.)*

ACTOR 5. Out of time Scrooge.

(Music: Cuts)

SCROOGE. *What!!?*

ACTOR 4. Final Curtain Scrooge!

(They grab **SCROOGE***'s hands. Swing him to face the audience.)*

SCROOGE. *No!!!!*

ACTORS. Smile Scrooge!

SCROOGE. No no no! Wait! Stop!

(The four **ACTORS** *burst into song.)*

(Music: "JOY TO THE WORLD")

(They march forward to take the curtain call, pulling **SCROOGE** *with them. Bow and back. Bow and back.* **SCROOGE** *drags back but they pull him on.)*

SCROOGE. Wait! No! Stop! It's not the end! It's not! Not the end! I want to – I want to – I want to LIVE!

(Sound Effect: Wild audience applause over music. Whoops and cheers.)

(The **ACTORS** *run back, run forward again,* **SCROOGE** *forced to run back and forth with them.)*

SCROOGE. No no no! Wait! Stop! It's not the end! It's not! Not the end! I want to live! Let me live! Let me live!!! *LET ME LIVE!!!* I beg of thee! I beg of thee spirit!!

(He struggles with the **ACTORS**. *He tries to escape but they are too strong for him. He keeps howling but in vain.)*

I beg of thee! I beg of thee! I beg of thee! I beg of –

(They overwhelm him. He vanishes from sight.)

(Lights: Blackout.)

(Music and Applause: Cuts)

(Lights: Fast Fade Up.)

Int. Scrooge's Bedroom, Christmas Day – Morning.

(SCROOGE is wrestling with his bed-sheet. His bedroom magically reappeared.)

SCROOGE. – thee! I beg of thee! I beg of thee! I beg of thee! I beg of –

(Silence. His face appears. He grabs the sheet. Looks at it.)

Wait! Thou art not a spirit! Thou art – a bedsheet!

(embraces the sheet) Dearest bedsheet! Lovely bedsheet! And look! My lovely bedposts! *(hugs the bedposts)* Lovely lovely bedposts! How I love thee bedposts! And – ah!! My lovely window! *(lovingly stroking window)* My lovely lovely window! With its lovely little Victorian window-catch. And its lovely view of Dickensian London! *(opens window, shouts out)* Hello there! Helloooo!

(A PASSER-BY enters.)

Look a lovely passer-by! Hello lovely Passer-by!

(PASSER-BY looks up, sees it is SCROOGE. Tries to run away.)

No wait! Dear sweet kind passer-by! Kindly tell me sir. What day is it pray?

PASSER-BY. Why Mr. Scr – Scrooge sir! What day sir? Why 'Tis – *(flinching)* – Christmas Day sir.

SCROOGE. Christmas Day!

PASSER-BY. Y – Y – Yes sir.

SCROOGE. But what year sir?

PASSER-BY. Y – Year sir? Four – fourteen eighty-two sir.

SCROOGE. *FOURTEEN EIGHTY-TWO!!??* Oh my God! I'm in Medieval England!

PASSER-BY. Eighteen forty-two sir! Sorry sir. My mistake sir.

SCROOGE. Christmas eighteen forty-two!???

PASSER-BY. Christmas eighteen forty-two sir! Yes sir!!!

SCROOGE. That's now isn't it? It's not the future?

PASSER-BY. Certainly not the future no sir! Certainly now sir. Now as it ever was sir! Never could it be no more now than it is now sir!

SCROOGE. Ah thank you thank you dear passer-by sir! Dear sweet good perfect passer-by!

PASSER-BY. Thank you Mr. Scrooge sir!

SCROOGE. I am alive!!! *(looks up to the heavens like Frankenstein's monster) I AM ALIVE!!!*

PASSER-BY. Oh my God!

*(***PASSER-BY*** runs for it. Bumps into the* **BOY IN STREET***.)*

BOY IN STREET. What's up?

SCROOGE. I'm in a play you know!!!

*(***BOY*** and* **PASSER-BY** *look blank.)*

All about me!

(points to the audience) That's the audience!!!

(bows and waves to the audience) Hellooo!

(if they wave back) They like me! Look! They like me! Hellooo! *(engages individual people)* How are you? Are you? Really!!? How marvellous! I am too. Who'd have thought it, eh? Ha ha ha!

PASSER-BY. He's gone barmy!

(Exits hurriedly. The **BOY** *about to run for it too.)*

SCROOGE. Dear boy, dear boy, wait wait I pray!

*(***BOY** *skids to a stop.)*

Tell me dear boy, dear dear boy in the street?

BOY IN STREET. Ye-ye-yessir?

SCROOGE. Would you know – dear sweet child – whether, by any chance, they've sold the prize turkey in the fine poulterer's in Pudding Lane?

BOY IN STREET. What the big white-feathered one as big as me sir?

SCROOGE. What a delightful sweet exceptional boy! Yes yes yes the big white feathered one as big as thee child.

BOY IN STREET. It's hanging there now sir!

SCROOGE. Ah! Heaven be praised! Then speedily speed thyself this instant and purchase that enormous great white bird as big as thee and tell 'em to bring it here, so that I may pay 'em and give 'em the direction where to deliver it. Do it in five minutes, I'll give you a shilling. Do it in less, I'll give you five!

BOY IN STREET. Five bob sir!! Blimey O'Reilly!! Right this minute sir!

(**BOY** *charges off. Scrooge's bedroom disappears.* **SCROOGE** *realises he's outside. He whoops with delight. He slides across the stage.*)

Ext. The Streets of London.
Christmas Day – Morning.

SCROOGE. Wheeeeeeee! I am as bright as a light and as light as a feather and as happy as an angel and as merry as a school-boy and as giddy and as dizzy as a drunken man.

(remembers the audience again, a florid bow) A Merry Christmas everybody! A Happy New Year to all the world!

(double takes) WHAT!!!!?? What did I just say!? Happy? Merry? Merry Christmas!!!?? I have never said Merry Christmas in all my life! All I ever said was hum – humbu – humbu –

(gasps) I can't say it! Hum – humbu – humbu – ha! 'Tis impossible to speak it!

(tries again) Humbu – humbu – humbu – Ha! Ha! Ha! What a wonder! Everything is a wonder! The world is a wonder! You are a wonder! I am a wonder! Christmas is a wonder! I love it! And –

(to audience) I love YOU! ALL of you!

(to individual person) And particularly *YOU* madam! D'you feel it too!? Isn't it – a miracle!!! *(sotto)* Are you doing anything later? *(loud)* What's come over me!? I need to dance!

(does a ballet leap) I need to sing!

(snatch of bel canto) La la la la la!!! I need to – dare I say it? – skate! Let's SKATE!!

(Music: "VOICES OF SPRING" – Johann Strauss)

(The other **ACTORS** *enter. They skate in formation towards* **SCROOGE** *as he pirouettes rather unsteadily, still in his nightcap and gown.)*

Wheeeeeeeeee! I'm skating and I don't care!!!

(They lead him round the stage in an elaborate skating routine. **SCROOGE** *is no expert, but what he loses in steadiness he makes up for in enthusiasm. At one point, he whizzes across the stage and disappears. Seconds later, he whizzes on from the opposite side, this time wearing a colorful scarf, a tall top hat and a splendid new overcoat, with his white night-shirt just peeking beneath it. Two* **SKATERS** *take him by the hands and swing him round, while the other two bring on a door with a Christmas wreath upon it. The first* **SKATERS** *deposit him at the door.)*

(Music: climaxes)

*(***ACTOR 3*** *becomes a* **HOUSEMAID***. She sees* **SCROOGE** *and shrieks.)*

SCROOGE. Sorry.

HOUSEMAID. Yes sir?

SCROOGE. Wouldst thy master be at er –

HOUSEMAID. Home sir?

SCROOGE. At home yes.

HOUSEMAID. Yes sir.

SCROOGE. Thanks anyway. I'll just er –

(He turns to go. Turns back.)

On the other hand –

(leaves again)

No no –

HOUSEMAID. Are you alright sir?

*(***SCROOGE** *turns back.)*

SCROOGE. Um – when you say – 'at home' you mean –

HOUSEMAID. At home sir.

SCROOGE. Right.

(She holds the door open. He plucks up the courage. Removes his top hat. Reveals the nightcap. Walks to the door.)

Thank you my dear.

(walks in)

Nice little hat by the way.

HOUSEMAID. Thank you sir. Nice little hat yourself sir.

(She curtsies.)

SCROOGE. Thank you too madam. *(curtsies too)*

Int. Frederick's Drawing Room – Christmas Day.

(FREDERICK and CONSTANCE enter. They stop transfixed. The HOUSEMAID stands staring too.)

FREDERICK. Bless my soul! Uncle –

SCROOGE. – Scrooge. 'Tis I. Indeed. Forgive my –
(adjusts his nightcap) – slightly erm unorthodox attire. I had a somewhat – disturbed night you might say. Anyway I just wondered – um – if – well – how to put this? *(retreating)* No no it is a bother. I can see. I am so sorry. Forgive me I –

CONSTANCE. You are welcome sir.

SCROOGE. Welcome?

CONSTANCE. You are always welcome uncle.

SCROOGE. Uncle? My – my dear Constance. I'm afraid we've never met. The blame lies with me. I have – I'm sorry to say – driven those away who might love me. I should explain – I – I – have been somewhat – haunted madam.

(Music: "THE BELLS OF ADELAIDE – ST CUTHBERTS [SPLICED SURPRISE MAJOR]" fade up in distance.)

CONSTANCE. There is nothing to explain sir. You are our family sir. The haunting is done sir.

SCROOGE. Family?

(ACTOR 2 enters. He is FREDERICK and CONSTANCE's CHILDREN.)

FREDERICK. These are our children by the way. All five of them.

SCROOGE. *(slight double-take)* Hello. Hello. Hello. Hello.
(one hiding) Hello.

CHILDREN. Hello.

SCROOGE. Um – might I ask – just – um – one tiny small question – um – will – there be – um – will there be –

FREDERICK. Christmas turkey uncle! Plum pudding uncle! Roast potatoes uncle! Chestnut stuffing and brussel sprouts and cranberry sauce and gravy and –

SCROOGE. Oh my goodness! Oh my goodness! Cranberry sauce! REAL GRAVY! How splendid! How magnificent! How unutterably marvellous! Indeed! But – um – forgive me – er – will – will –will – there be – um – I cannot ask –

FREDERICK. Ask uncle.

SCROOGE. *(small voice)* – games?

FREDERICK. Games uncle! Wonderful games! Wonderful merry games uncle!!

(Music: BELLS SEGUE INTO:)

(Music: "FANTASIA ON CHRISTMAS CAROLS" – Vaughan Williams: 'LAST MOVEMENT [God Bless the Ruler of this House & Sussex Carol')

[Please note: If V. Williams Fantasia version is not available, ACTORS 2 and 4 and later ACTORS 3 and 5 could sing the two carols interweaving behind the scene.]

HOUSEMAID. *(sings)*
ON CHRISTMAS NIGHT ALL PEOPLE SING
TO HEAR THE NEWS THE ANGELS BRING

FREDERICK. Merry Christmas uncle.

CHILDREN. *(sings)*
NEWS OF GREAT JOY, NEWS OF GREAT MIRTH. NEWS OF OUR MERCIFUL KING'S BIRTH.

SCROOGE. Say that again please?

HOUSEMAID. *(sings)*
WHEN SIN DEPARTS BEFORE THY GRACE THEN LIFE AND HEALTH COME IN IT'S PLACE.

CONSTANCE. Merry Christmas Uncle Ebenezer!

(She hugs him. He freezes with ancient terror, but she holds on.)

FREDERICK. Merry Christmas Uncle Ebenezer

(FREDERICK hugs SCROOGE too. FREDERICK and CONSTANCE hold him together. The CHILDREN and HOUSEMAID join too. They all hug SCROOGE. 'Til SCROOGE slowly but surely melts. He hugs them back. They dance round laughing.)

SCROOGE. Oh merry Christmas! Merry Christmas! Merry Christmas! Merry Christmas!

ALL. Merry Christmas! Merry Christmas! Merry Christmas! Merry Christmas!

FREDERICK. *(sings)*
GOD BLESS THE RULER OF THIS HOUSE AND LONG ON MAY
HE REIGN.

HOUSEMAID. *(sings)*
FROM OUT OF DARKNESS WE HAVE LIGHT WHICH MAKES
THE ANGELS SING THIS NIGHT.

CONSTANCE. *(sings)*
MANY HAPPY CHRISTMASES HE LIVE TO SEE AGAIN.

CHILDREN. *(sing)*
FROM OUT OF DARKNESS WE HAVE LIGHT WHICH MAKES
THE ANGELS SING THIS NIGHT

FREDERICK. *(sings)*
GOD BLESS OUR GENERATION WHO LIVE BOTH FAR AND
NEAR.

HOUSEMAID. *(sings)*
GLORY TO GOD AND PEACE TO MEN.

ALL. *(sing)*
AND WE WISH THEM A HAPPY, A HAPPY NEW YEAR.

HOUSEMAID. *(sings)*
BOTH NOW AND EVERMORE. AMEN.

ALL. *(sing)*
GOD BLESS THE RULER OF THIS HOUSE AND LONG ON MAY
HE REIGN
MANY HAPPY CHRISTMASES HE LIVE TO SEE AGAIN
GOD BLESS OUR GENERATION WHO LIVE BOTH FAR AND
NEAR
AND WE WISH THEM A HAPPY, A HAPPY NEW YEAR
OH WE WISH YOU A HAPPY, A HAPPY NEW YEAR.

HOUSEMAID. *(sings)*

BOTH NOW AND EVERMORE. AMEN.

(As the **ACTORS** *and* **SCROOGE** *sing this last verse, they spin on stage, while snow-flakes fall from the flies.)*

(Music: fades)

(The **ACTORS** *spin off stage, leaving* **SCROOGE** *spinning alone beneath the snow-flakes. He spins slowly to a stop. The final snow-flakes fall.)*

Int. Scrooge's Counting House – Boxing Day.

(CRATCHIT enters. He creeps in. SCROOGE does not move but watches him sternly. He puts on his black top hat. Pulls up the collar of his big black coat.)

SCROOGE. *Cratchit!*

(CRATCHIT freezes.)

I've had enough of this lateness Cratchit.

CRATCHIT. Yes sir.

SCROOGE. So I'll tell you what I'm going to do Cratchit.

CRATCHIT. Yes sir.

SCROOGE. I am going to –

(CRATCHIT waits for the axe to fall.)

CRATCHIT. Yes sir?

SCROOGE. – raise your salary Bob!

(CRATCHIT freezes.)

SCROOGE. Twenty times! Thirty times Bob! Forty times! Fifty times! Oh Bob! Bob! Bob! My dear dear dearest Bob!

(He rushes to hug him. CRATCHIT shrieks, puts his fists up.)

CRATCHIT. Keep away sir, please sir beggin' yer pardon sir!

(SCROOGE tries to hug him again. CRATCHIT crawls through his legs. Runs to the other side of stage.)

CRATCHIT. *KEEP AWAY SIR KEEP AWAY SIR!* Or I shall be forced to call for a straight-waistcoat and a big lady nurse from the Bedlam hospital sir!

SCROOGE. Tell me dearest Bob. Did you receive a mysterious turkey yesterday?

CRATCHIT. Turkey sir? We did sir! *(gasps)* So it was – from *you* sir? Oh sir! It was bigger than Tiny Tim sir! Oh sorry sir, Tiny Tim is my little –

SCROOGE. I know who he is Bob.

CRATCHIT. You do sir?

SCROOGE. And how is Tiny Tim Bob?

CRATCHIT. With such fine good nourishment as that sir, we have every hope for him sir!

SCROOGE. Thank the lord indeed dearest Bob! And Bob?

CRATCHIT. Yes sir?

SCROOGE. My box of money. It is still here?

CRATCHIT. Indeed it is sir.

SCROOGE. Then let us unlock it Bob and take its contents, that have enchained and enslaved me through my greed and selfishness even to the very point of death, and let me who hath distribute all of it to all of them who hath not.

CRATCHIT. Very good sir!

SCROOGE. And we shall rid this world of the shackles of profit and greed! Of all owings and lendings and interests and borrowings and loans and penalties and bonuses and all other wretched devices that make one richer by making another poorer. I shall devote my life to it Bob. To make the world a good and kind and fair and happy place for all. And Bob?

CRATCHIT. Yes sir?

SCROOGE. I wonder – might I come to visit thy family Bob? And read to Tiny Tim? Read him – *Ali Baba*?

CRATCHIT. Oh sir! *Ali Baba* sir! Yes sir! That would be a treasure sir, the greatest treasure ever sir. Or may I say – a blessing sir.

SCROOGE. Blessing Bob?

(SCROOGE clutches his heart. Starts to gasp.)

Bob! Bob!

CRATCHIT. What is it sir!? What is it!?

SCROOGE. My heart Bob!

CRATCHIT. *(alarmed)* Your heart sir!? Your heart!!?

SCROOGE. 'Tis – 'tis – *(listens, laughs)* – beating Bob! 'Tis beating! Listen Bob! Canst hear it?

CRATCHIT. *(leans in to listen)* Oh yes sir! I can sir!

SCROOGE. But listen Bob listen! Not only my heart dost thou hear. But every heart. Every heart in every part of all the world Bob. All beating together. As one great family. For that is what we are, is it not sir? A great family! Sharing the great journey of this life and the great blessing of this great rolling earth. All of us together sir! Are we not Mr Cratchit sir? Are we not sir?

CRATCHIT. Oh yes Mr Scrooge sir, indeed we are sir! A great family! Journeying all together sir! Sharing the blessing of this great rolling earth and no mistake sir. Open Sesame sir! Open Sesame!

(Music: "BRITTEN – NOYES FLUDDE: The Spacious Firmament on High. 0:00 – 0:27")

EPILOGUE

ACTOR 2. Indeed Ebenezer Scrooge was even better than his word. And he became as good a friend, as good a benefactor, as good an uncle and as good a man as good old England ever knew.

ACTOR 4. And from that day he had no further need for spirits, but lived upon the Total Abstinence Principal ever afterwards.

ACTOR 3. And past, present and future lived within him as one time. And as for Christmas –

ACTOR 5. – it was said of him ever after that he knew how to keep Christmas as well and true as any man alive.

ACTOR 2. As a time for giving and for blessing. And for love.

SCROOGE. And so, as Tiny Tim observed –

(**ACTOR 2** *reveals* **TINY TIM**. **SCROOGE** *puts him on his shoulder.*)

TINY TIM. God Bless us each and all and every one!

(**ACTOR 3** *runs off and hurtles back with the phonograph and trumpet. He winds it. It plays. Not tinny this time but full-bodied sound. The* **COMPANY** *join in as they sing:*)

(*Music: "HALLELUJAH CHORUS – MESSIAH: HANDEL"*)

(*The* **ACTORS** *link hands with* **SCROOGE** *and run on for the true curtain call. Democratic at last, no master, no servants, all of them together, they sing with the audience:*)

(*MUSIC: "DING DONG MERRILY ON HIGH", "GOD REST YE MERRY GENTLEMEN", "WE WISH YOU A MERRY CHRISTMAS", "HERE WE COME A'WASSAILING"*)

ALTERNATIVE ENDING

This is a final verse to the song "HARD TIMES OF OLD ENGLAND" that we heard sung by the people of England on Kennington Common. I always wanted this at the end of the show (linking as it does to the earlier scene, to Dickens's passion for social justice and of course to burning issues of our own time) and so it remained until the last preview when pre-first night nerves got the better of everyone and the song was deemed not Christmassy enough or something, I forget what exactly, so I agreed to cut it. With regret. I offer it again in this edition to directors and companies with the chutzpah to do it.

ACTORS.
> GOOD PEOPLE WE'RE SINGING I HOPE YOU CAN SEE,
> WE'VE HAD SOME HARD TIMES BUT THEY DON'T HAVE TO
> BE
> WE'LL BUILD A NEW WORLD IS IT TOO MUCH TO DREAM
> TOGETHER WE'LL BUILD A NEW ENGLAND
> A NEW WORLD FOR YOU AND FOR ME.
> YES A NEW WORLD FOR YOU AND FOR ME.
> YE-ES A NEW WORLD FOR YOU AND FOR ME!!!

The End

ABOUT THE PLAYWRIGHT

Besides *A Christmas Carol*, PATRICK BARLOW is renowned for his four-person adaptation of *The 39 Steps* which has played in over forty countries world-wide. It has won Olivier, Helpmann Moliere and Tony Awards and made Patrick the most performed playwright in America for 2012. Patrick is celebrated in the UK for his two-man theatre company National Theatre of Brent, whose comedy epics include *Wagner's Ring Cycle, The Charles and Diana Story, The Messiah, The Wonder of Sex, The Arts and How They Was Done, The Black Hole of Calcutta, The Life and Times of the Dalai Lama* and *Zulu!* They have won two Sony Gold Awards, a Premier Ondas Award for Best European Comedy and the New York Festival Gold Award for Best Comedy. Other screenwriting includes *Van Gogh* (Prix Futura Berlin Film Festival), *Revolution!!* (Best Comedy Jerusalem Film Festival) and the BAFTA-winning *Young Visiters*. Publications include *Shakespeare: The Truth!* and *The Complete History of the Whole World*. Patrick has also appeared in *Absolutely Fabulous, Shakespeare in Love, Notting Hill, Nanny McPhee* and *The Diary of Bridget Jones*. On stage he has appeared as Pseudolus in *A Funny Thing Happened On the Way to the Forum,* Truscott in Joe Orton's *Loot,* Humphry in Simon Gray's *The Common Pursuit* and Toad in the Royal National Theatre's *The Wind in the Willows*. He is currently writing two further four-person epics, *Ben-Hur* and *The Hound of the Baskervilles*.